核心 素養 108課綱

讀出英語

核心素養 ②

九大技巧打造閱讀力

跨領域主題 ╳ 生活化體裁 ╳ 250道閱讀題

高效培養核心素養

精準貼合108 課綱

用英語打造閱讀、分析、整合力！

作者● Owain Mckimm　　譯者●劉嘉珮　　審訂● Helen Yeh

協同作者● Zachary Fillingham

Contents

Unit 1 Reading Skills 閱讀技巧

體裁 / 主題	議題	素養
poem 詩 / arts & literature 藝術與文學	reading literacy 閱讀素養教育	artistic appreciation 藝術涵養
interview 訪談 / culture 文化	multiculturalism 多元文化教育	cultural understanding 多元文化
passage 文章 / architecture 建築	multiculturalism 多元文化教育	aesthetic literacy 美感素養
poster 海報 / school life 學校生活	human rights 人權教育	citizenship 公民意識
passage 文章 / health & body 健康與身體	security 安全教育	physical and mental wellness 身心素質
magazine article 雜誌文章 / customs & lifestyles 風俗與生活方式	multiculturalism 多元文化教育	aesthetic literacy 美感素養
card 卡片 / everyday life 日常生活	family education 家庭教育	interpersonal relationship 人際關係
advertisements 廣告 / everyday life 日常生活	information 資訊教育	information and technology literacy 科技資訊
passage 文章 / holidays & festivals 假日與節日	multiculturalism 多元文化教育	cultural understanding 多元文化
group chat 多人聊天 / school life 學校生活	career planning 生涯規劃教育	teamwork 團隊合作

體裁 / 主題	議題	素養
email 電子郵件 / everyday life 日常生活	morality 品德教育	interpersonal relationship 人際關係
passage 文章 / nature 自然	environment 環境教育	citizenship 公民意識
website 網站 / environment 環境	environment 環境教育	citizenship 公民意識
passage 文章 / social behavior 社會行為	information 資訊教育	information and technology literacy 科技資訊
news clip transcript 新聞短片字稿 / environment 環境	environment 環境教育	citizenship 公民意識
conversation 對話 / inspiration for teens 青少年啟發	morality 品德教育	moral praxis 道德實踐
passage 文章 / social behavior 社會行為	information 資訊教育	media literacy 媒體素養
flyer 傳單 / animals 動物	life 生命教育	moral praxis 道德實踐
magazine article 雜誌文章 / gender equality 性別平等	gender equality 性別平等教育	global understanding 國際理解
diary 日記 / inspiration for teens 青少年啟發	human rights 人權教育	problem solving 解決問題
column 專欄 / society 社會	life 生命教育	citizenship 公民意識
book foreword 書本前言 / culture 文化	multiculturalism 多元文化教育	cultural understanding 多元文化
video call 視訊通話 / health & body 健康與身體	international education 國際教育	global understanding 國際理解
notice 通知 / school life 學校生活	international education 國際教育	global understanding 國際理解

Unit 3　Study Strategies 學習策略

體裁 / 主題	議題	素養
passage 文章 / language & communication 語言與溝通	reading literacy 閱讀素養教育	expression 溝通表達
notice 通知 / animals 動物	environment 環境教育	citizenship 公民意識
passage 文章 / animals 動物	environment 環境教育	citizenship 公民意識
passage 文章 / places 景點	multiculturalism 多元文化教育	cultural understanding 多元文化
diary 日記 / career 職涯	security 安全教育	self-advancement 自我精進
speech 演說 / phenomenon 現象	morality 品德教育	expression 溝通表達
calendar 行事曆 / career 職涯	career planning 生涯規劃教育	innovation and adaptation 創新應變
map 地圖 / geography 地理	outdoor education 戶外教育	global understanding 國際理解
line graph 折線圖 / technology 科技	career planning 生涯規劃教育	information and technology literacy 科技資訊
bar graph 長條圖 / career 職涯	career planning 生涯規劃教育	planning and execution 規劃執行
pie chart 圓餅圖 / environment 環境	environment 環境教育	citizenship 公民意識
table of contents 目錄 / everyday life 日常生活	reading literacy 閱讀素養教育	physical and mental wellness 身心素質
timeline 時間軸 / computer 電腦	information 資訊教育	information and technology literacy 科技資訊
recipe 食譜 / food & drinks 食物與飲料	reading literacy 閱讀素養教育	planning and execution 規劃執行

體裁 / 主題	議題	素養
thesaurus 同義詞典 / language & communication 語言與溝通	reading literacy 閱讀素養教育	semiotics 符號運用
website 網站 / entertainment 環境	information 資訊教育	media literacy 媒體素養
passage 文章 / famous or interesting people 知名或有趣的人物	multiculturalism 多元文化教育	global understanding 國際理解
website 網站 / health & body 健康與身體	international education 國際教育	citizenship 公民意識
passage 文章 / science 科學	reading literacy 閱讀素養教育	logical thinking 系統思考
passage 文章 + bullet points 列點 / plants 植物	environment 環境教育	planning and execution 規劃執行
passage 文章 / sport 體育	security 安全教育	teamwork 團隊合作
website 網站 / inspiration for teens 青少年啟發	career planning 生涯規劃教育	self-advancement 自我精進
interview 訪談 / career 職涯	career planning 生涯規劃教育	self-advancement 自我精進
website 網站 / food & drinks 食物與飲料	reading literacy 閱讀素養教育	information and technology literacy 科技資訊
Venn diagram 文氏圖 / animals 動物	environment 環境教育	logical thinking 系統思考
index 索引 / language & communication 語言與溝通	reading literacy 閱讀素養教育	semiotics 符號運用

Introduction

本套書共四冊，專為英語初學者設計，旨在**增進閱讀理解能力**並**提升閱讀技巧**。全套書符合 108 課綱要旨，強調**跨領域**、**生活化學習**，文章按照教育部公布的**九大核心素養**與 **19 項議題設計**撰寫，為讀者打造扎實的英語閱讀核心素養能力。

每冊內含 50 篇文章，主題包羅萬象，包括**文化**、**科學**、**自然**、**文學**等，內容以**日常生活常見體裁**寫成，舉凡**電子郵件**、**邀請函**、**廣告**、**公告**、**對話**皆收錄於書中，以多元主題及多變體裁，豐富讀者閱讀體驗，引導讀者從生活中學習，並將學習運用於生活。每篇文章之後設計**五道閱讀理解題**，依不同閱讀技巧重點精心撰寫，訓練統整、分析及應用所得資訊的能力，同時為日後的國中教育會考做準備。

Key Features 本書特色

1. 按文章難度分級，可依程度選用適合的級數

全套書難度不同，方便各程度的學生使用，以文章字數、高級字詞使用數、文法難度、句子長度分為一至四冊，如下方表格所示：

文章字數 （每篇）	國中 1200 字 （每篇）	國中 1201-2000 字 （每篇）	高中字彙 （3-5 級）（每篇）	文法	句子最長字數
Book 1 120-150	93%	7 字	3 字	國一	15 字
Book 2 150-180	86%	15 字	6 字	國二	18 字
Book 3 180-210	82%	30 字	7 字	國三	25 字
Book 4 210-250	75%	50 字	12 字	進階	28 字

2. 按文章難度分級，可依程度選用適合的級數

全書**主題多元**，有**青少年生活、家庭、娛樂、環境、健康、節慶、文化、動物、文學、旅遊**等，帶領讀者以英語探索知識、豐富生活，同時拉近學習與日常的距離。

3. 文章體裁豐富多樣

廣納各類生活中**常見的體裁**，包含**短文、詩篇、對話、廣告、傳單、新聞、短片、專欄**等，讓讀者學會閱讀多種體裁文章，將閱讀知識及能力應用於生活中。

4. 外師親錄課文朗讀 MP3

全書文章皆由專業外師錄製 MP3，示範正確發音，促進讀者聽力吸收，提升英文聽力與口說能力。

Structure of the Book | 本書架構

Unit 1 閱讀技巧 Reading Skills

本單元訓練讀者**理解文意**的基本技巧，內容包含：

1 **歸納要旨／找出支持性細節 Main Ideas / Supporting Details**

要旨是文章傳達的關鍵訊息，也就是作者想要講述的重點。一般而言，只要看前幾句就能大略掌握文章的要旨。

支持性細節就像是築起房屋的磚塊，幫助讀者逐步了解整篇文章要旨，**事實**、**描述**、**比較**、**舉例**都能是支持性細節的一種。

2 **作者的目的及語氣／做出推測**
Author's Purpose and Tone / Making Inferences

作者通常在寫作時有特定的**目的**，他可能是想博君一笑，或是引發你對某個主題深思。注意作者的**語氣**，他的語氣是詼諧、情感充沛亦或是有耐心的呢？作者的語氣可以幫助你找出作者的目的。

當你在進行**推測**時，需使用已知的資訊去推論出不熟悉的資訊。在篇章的上下文中，讀者藉由文中已提供的資訊去推測文意。

3 **理解因果關係／釐清寫作技巧 Cause and Effect / Clarifying Devices**

一起事件通常都有發生的**原因**與造成的**結果**，讀者可以從文章內的 **because of**（由於）、**as a result of**（因而）等片語找出原因，並從 **as a result**（結果，不加 of）、**resulting in**（因此）和 **so**（所以）等片語得知結果。

作者會想讓自己的文章盡量引人入勝且文意明瞭。當你在閱讀時，需注意作者用哪些技巧達到此目的。看看作者是否提供事實及數據？是否向讀者提問？是否舉出例證？仔細閱讀每個句子及段落，試著分辨**寫作技巧**。

Unit 2 | 字彙學習 Word Study

本單元訓練讀者擴充字彙量，並學會了解文章中的生字，內容包含：

❶ 同義詞與反義詞 Synonyms / Antonyms

在英文中有時兩字的意思相近，此時稱這兩字為**同義詞**；若兩字意思完全相反，則稱為**反義詞**。舉例來說，good（好）和 brilliant（很棒）的意思相近，為同義詞，但 good（好）和 bad（壞）的意思相反，故為反義詞。學習這些詞彙有助提升字彙量，並增進閱讀與寫作能力。

❷ 從上下文推測字義 Words In Context

遇到不會的英文字，就算是跟它大眼瞪小眼，也無法了解其字義，但若好好觀察此字的**上下文**，或許就能推敲出大略的字義。這項技巧十分重要，尤其有助讀者在閱讀文章時，即使遇到不會的生字，也能選出正確答案。

Unit 3 | 學習策略 Study Strategies

影像圖表與**參考資料**常會附在文章旁，幫助讀者獲得許多額外重點，本單元引導讀者善用文章中的不同素材來蒐集資訊，內容包含：

❶ 影像圖表 Visual Material

影像圖表可以將複雜資訊轉換成簡單的**表格、圖表、地圖**等，是閱讀時的最佳幫手。要讀懂圖表，首先要閱讀**圖表標題與單位**，接著觀察**數值**，只要理解圖表的架構，就能從中得到重要資訊。

❷ 參考資料 Reference Sources

參考資料像是**字典、書籍索引**等，一次呈現大量資訊，能訓練讀者自行追蹤所需重點的能力，並提升讀者對文章的整體理解。

Unit 4 | 綜合練習 Final Reviews

本單元綜合前三單元內容，幫助讀者回顧全書所學，並藉由文後綜合習題，來檢視自身吸收程度。

How to Use This Book

1 多樣主題增添閱讀樂趣與知識

環境

UNIT 1 (13)

13

» cleaning the beach

Keeping the Coast Clean

Clean-Up at White Sand Beach

Details   **Event by:** Maggie Wang

📍 White Sand Beach

🕐 Monday, June 3 from 8 a.m. to 11 a.m.

👥 15 people are currently going.

1   Come and help us keep White Sand Beach clean! White Sand Beach is a wonderful place. People love to relax or play beach games on the sand. And it is a very popular place for children to run around and play. However, there is currently a lot of trash on the beach. There are bottles, plastic bags, paper cups, and candy wrappers. We want the beach to be a clean, safe place for everyone to enjoy. So we are looking for volunteers to come and help us pick up the trash on the beach.

2   We will provide you with trash bags and gloves. We will also provide snacks and drinks. All you need to bring is yourself and a helpful attitude (and maybe a hat, as it will be a sunny day)!

3   We will meet outside the beach café at 8 a.m. We look forward to seeing you there!

044

文化

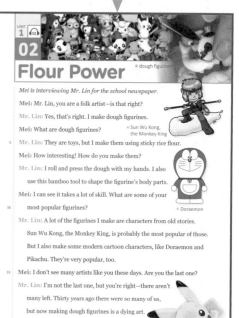

UNIT 1 (02)

02

Flour Power

» dough figurines

Mei is interviewing Mr. Lin for the school newspaper.

Mei: Mr. Lin, you are a folk artist—is that right?

Mr. Lin: Yes, that's right. I make dough figurines.

Mei: What are dough figurines?

» Sun Wu Kong, the Monkey King

5   **Mr. Lin:** They are toys, but I make them using sticky rice flour.

Mei: How interesting! How do you make them?

Mr. Lin: I roll and press the dough with my hands. I also use this bamboo tool to shape the figurine's body parts.

Mei: I can see it takes a lot of skill. What are some of your

10   most popular figurines?

» Doraemon

Mr. Lin: A lot of the figurines I make are characters from old stories. Sun Wu Kong, the Monkey King, is probably the most popular of those. But I also make some modern cartoon characters, like Doraemon and Pikachu. They're very popular, too.

15   **Mei:** I don't see many artists like you these days. Are you the last one?

Mr. Lin: I'm not the last one, but you're right—there aren't many left. Thirty years ago there were so many of us, but now making dough figurines is a dying art.

Mei: Mr. Lin, thank you for speaking with me.

022

» Pikachu

動物

UNIT 1 (18)

18 Our Animals Need You!

Our Animals Need You!

1   Do you love animals? Are you over the age of 18? Do you have at least three hours of free time a week?

2   At the **Safe Home Animals Shelter** we are looking for helpers.

3   We currently house over fifty dogs and cats, and they need lots of care and attention. We need people to help with different jobs around the shelter. These include:

>> Feeding our animals

>> Keeping our shelter clean

>> Walking the dogs

>> Playing with the cats

>> Giving some of the animals medicine

>> Posting about our animals on social media

4   **Please note:**

Our shelter does not make any money, so we are not able to pay our helpers. But we can promise that the work is very rewarding. In return for your help, you will get lots of love from our wonderful animals.

5   If you think this is something you would like to do, please call us on 555-345-234 and leave your information. We will call you back if we think you would be good as one of our helpers.

054

2 多元體裁貼近日常閱讀體驗

對話

詩篇

網頁

UNIT 1 · 16

» older adults

16 A Question for the Class

A teacher asked her students a question. Here's how they responded:

Julia: I often see young children using them. I don't think they should because they are young and have a lot of energy. I think only old people, disabled people, and pregnant women should be able to use them. 5

⌃ disabled person

Mark: I think they should be available for anyone who needs them. I often feel sick on buses and trains and need to sit down. Once I was really ill and one was empty. But I didn't sit because I thought people would shout at me. 10

Kim: I disagree with Mark. If you said anyone could use them, then people would take advantage of the system. For example, people could give silly excuses like "I need to sit because I have a heavy bag." I think the system is fine the way it is. 15

⌃ pregnant woman

Gregg: I think we should get rid of them altogether. Most people are kind. They would always give up a seat if they saw that someone needed it. Having them just puts pressure on people. 20

050

UNIT 1 · 01

01 The Woman in the Famous Painting

1 *At first I could only catch glimpses*
of you through the museum crowd.
You were smaller than I expected,
and darker—all greens, yellows and browns.
Nothing special, I thought.

2 *But then I got closer, and I could see your eyes.*
They seemed to follow me from side to side,
as if you were alive and interested in me!
My heart began to beat.

⌃ Mona Lisa

3 *And then I was in front of you, and there it was—*
your famous smile! But were you smiling?
I wasn't sure. I looked away, and back again,
And now you seemed to look a little sad,
like you were forcing that smile, for us.
Day after day after day after day.

4 *And then, I knew.*
That look in your eyes—it wasn't interest.
It was boredom. It was the desire to slip into a dream.
And in that world of dreams you might be free—
no frame, no millions of staring eyes.
And there, perhaps, you'd smile for real.

5 *I could only imagine how beautiful that smile would be.*

020

UNIT 4 · 48

48

100 Delicious Dishes in One Book

Rich Logan's Delicious Dishes
by Rich Logan
★ ★ ★ ★ ★

Over 100 delicious recipes from the winner of the TV show "SuperChef."

Buy Now $15.99

Reviews

"Every serious home cook should own this book!"
— *Home Cook Magazine*

"Rich Logan knows how to make simple ingredients taste delicious!"
— *Food World*

"This book contains dishes from all over the world—France, China, India, Italy, the UK, and many more. If you want to learn to cook a wide range of dishes, this book is for you!"
— *Daily News Book Reviews*

"Each recipe in this book uses a simple list of ingredients and is easy to follow. So it is perfect for beginners. But experienced cooks will also learn some cool new tricks as well."
— *Good Food Monthly*

"These dishes will be familiar to experienced cooks, but Logan puts his own special twist on each one. Even though I am a long-time cook, I was still excited to try out each recipe."
— *Darius Brown, Head Chef at the Prince Restaurant, London*

120

___ 1. What is the main point of the interview?

(A) Mr. Lin makes dough figurines with sticky rice flour.

(B) Sun Wu Kong is one of Mr. Lin's most popular figurines.

(C) The interviewer thinks Mr. Lin's figurines are highly interesting.

(D) Making dough figurines is a dying art.

❶ 歸納要旨

___ 2. Which of the following does Mr. Lin use to make his dough figurines?

(A) A bamboo tool.　(B) A toy.　(C) Noodles.　(D) Scissors.

❷ 找出支持性細節

_____ 1. What is the purpose of this magazine article?

(A) To give an answer to a difficult problem.

(B) To point out something terrible.

(C) To explain the history of something.

(D) To present something interesting.

❸ 作者的目的及語氣

_____ 3. What is probably TRUE about Gillian Grey?

(A) She never wears steampunk fashion.

(B) She doesn't know what steampunk fashion is.

(C) She is a big fan of steampunk clothes.

(D) She designs steampunk fashion herself.

❹ 做出推測

_____ 3. Why is the event in the reading happening?

(A) There is a lot of trash on the beach.

(B) People love to relax on the beach.

(C) Monday, June 3 will be very sunny.

(D) Fifteen people are currently going.

❺ 理解因果關係

_____ 4. How does the writer end the second paragraph?

(A) With a play on words.　　(B) With a sad story.

(C) With a piece of advice.　　(D) With an example.

❻ 釐清寫作技巧

___ 1. What is another word for "conversation"?

(A) Talk.　(B) Computer.　(C) Problem.　(D) Person.

❼ 了解同義字

___ 2. What is the opposite of "powerful"?

(A) Strong.　(B) Loud.　(C) Difficult.　(D) Weak.

❽ 了解反義字

___ 3. What does the writer mean by "empty words"?

(A) Words with difficult spelling.

(B) Words with no meaning.

(C) Words nobody understands.

(D) Words in a foreign language.

❾ 從上下文推測字義

4 各式圖表與全彩圖片促進閱讀理解

地圖

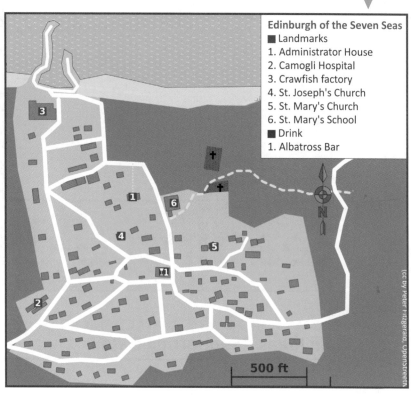

Edinburgh of the Seven Seas
■ Landmarks
1. Administrator House
2. Camogli Hospital
3. Crawfish factory
4. St. Joseph's Church
5. St. Mary's Church
6. St. Mary's School
■ Drink
1. Albatross Bar

(cc by Peter Fitzgerald, Openstreets)

500 ft

圖片

折線圖

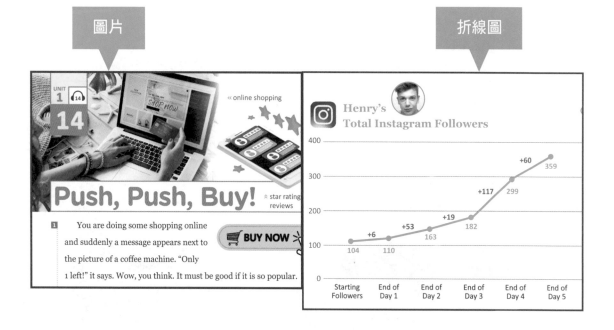

« online shopping

UNIT 1 14

14

Push, Push, Buy!

☆ star rating reviews

1 You are doing some shopping online and suddenly a message appears next to the picture of a coffee machine. "Only 1 left!" it says. Wow, you think. It must be good if it is so popular.

BUY NOW

Henry's
Total Instagram Followers

+6
+53
+19
+117
+60

104
110
163
182
299
359

Starting Followers | End of Day 1 | End of Day 2 | End of Day 3 | End of Day 4 | End of Day 5

UNIT
1

Reading Skills

This unit covers six key elements you will need to focus on in order to properly understand an article: main idea(s), supporting details, author's purpose and tone, making inferences, cause and effect, and clarifying devices.

In this unit, you will learn how to understand what a text is mainly about, observe how details support main ideas, pinpoint the reason behind an author's writing, make assumptions based on information in the text, recognize connections between events, and identify the way a writer makes their work interesting.

01 The Woman in the Famous Painting

1 *At first I could only catch glimpses*
of you through the museum crowd.
You were smaller than I expected,
and darker—all greens, yellows and browns.
Nothing special, I thought.

2 *But then I got closer, and I could see your eyes.*
They seemed to follow me from side to side,
as if you were alive and interested in me!
My heart began to beat.

⌃ *Mona Lisa*

3 *And then I was in front of you, and there it was—*
your famous smile! But were you smiling?
I wasn't sure. I looked away, and back again,
And now you seemed to look a little sad,
like you were forcing that smile, for us.
Day after day after day after day.

4 *And then, I knew.*
That look in your eyes—it wasn't interest.
It was boredom. It was the desire to slip into a dream.
And in that world of dreams you might be free—
no frame, no millions of staring eyes.
And there, perhaps, you'd smile for real.

5 *I could only imagine how beautiful that smile would be.*

QUESTIONS

_____ 1. **What is the main idea of the poem?**
(A) The writer visited a museum and saw a famous painting for the first time.
(B) The writer understood something special about a famous painting.
(C) Many people come to the museum to see the painting in the poem.
(D) The painting in the poem was smaller than the writer expected.

_____ 2. **What is the main point of the third verse/paragraph?**
(A) The painting hangs in the museum every day.
(B) The writer noticed the smile of the person in the painting.
(C) The person in the painting is smiling but doesn't seem happy.
(D) The writer finally got to stand in front of the famous painting.

_____ 3. **What is special about the eyes of the person in the painting?**
(A) They are large and beautiful.   (B) They are closed.
(C) They are bright blue.   (D) They seem to move.

_____ 4. **What is TRUE about the painting?**
(A) It shows a person that is crying.
(B) It is famous for its smiling subject.
(C) It is not popular among museum visitors.
(D) The painting is black and white.

_____ 5. **On the wall next to the painting, the author found the information on the right. Which of the following is NOT true about the painting?**
(A) The painting is less than 100 years old.
(B) A man named Leonardo da Vinci painted it.
(C) The painter used oil paints to create the painting.
(D) The painting is less than one meter tall.

Title:
Mona Lisa
Painter:
Leonardo da Vinci
Year:
1503-1506
Size:
77 cm × 53 cm
Type of paint:
Oil

^ dough figurines

02
Flour Power

Mei is interviewing Mr. Lin for the school newspaper.

Mei: Mr. Lin, you are a folk artist—is that right?

Mr. Lin: Yes, that's right. I make dough figurines.

Mei: What are dough figurines?

» Sun Wu Kong, the Monkey King

5 **Mr. Lin:** They are toys, but I make them using sticky rice flour.

Mei: How interesting! How do you make them?

Mr. Lin: I roll and press the dough with my hands. I also

use this bamboo tool to shape the figurine's body parts.

Mei: I can see it takes a lot of skill. What are some of your

10 most popular figurines?

^ Doraemon

Mr. Lin: A lot of the figurines I make are characters from old stories.

Sun Wu Kong, the Monkey King, is probably the most popular of those.

But I also make some modern cartoon characters, like Doraemon and

Pikachu. They're very popular, too.

15 **Mei:** I don't see many artists like you these days. Are you the last one?

Mr. Lin: I'm not the last one, but you're right—there aren't

many left. Thirty years ago there were so many of us,

but now making dough figurines is a dying art.

Mei: Mr. Lin, thank you for speaking with me.

» Pikachu

QUESTIONS

_____1. **What is the main point of the interview?**
   (A) Mr. Lin makes dough figurines with sticky rice flour.
   (B) Sun Wu Kong is one of Mr. Lin's most popular figurines.
   (C) The interviewer thinks Mr. Lin's figurines are highly interesting.
   (D) Making dough figurines is a dying art.

_____2. **Which of the following does Mr. Lin use to make his dough figurines?**
   (A) A bamboo tool.   (B) A toy.   (C) Noodles.   (D) Scissors.

_____3. **Which of the following is NOT true about Mr. Lin's figurines?**
   (A) Many of them are from old stories.
   (B) Pikachu is a popular character.
   (C) Some are from modern-day cartoons.
   (D) Some look like modern-day pop stars.

_____4. **What is TRUE about artists like Mr. Lin?**
   (A) Thirty years ago there weren't many of them around.
   (B) Thirty years ago there were fewer than there are today.
   (C) There are much fewer now than there were thirty years ago.
   (D) There were none thirty years ago, but now there are many.

_____5. **The announcement below appeared in the school newspaper after an article about Mr. Lin.**

Learn to Make Dough Figurines!
With Mr. Lin

Friday, March 10, 4 p.m.– 6 p.m. in Art Room B

Learn a cool Taiwanese folk art!

You'll learn to make all kinds of cool characters, from Sun Wu Kong to Pikachu!

Class size: Maximum 20 people.

. . . .

Sign up at the reception desk.
For students of Jinshan Junior High School <u>only</u>.

What is the main message of the ad?
(A) Mr. Lin will hold a special class to teach students how to make dough figurines.
(B) Only students of Jinshan Junior High School can attend Mr. Lin's class.
(C) No more than 20 students can attend Mr. Lin's class.
(D) The class will take place in Art Room B on the evening of Friday, March 10.

03 A Mosque Like No Other

1   The town of Djenné in Mali is home to one of the most unique religious buildings in the world. Its name is the Great Mosque of Djenné. What makes the building so unique? While most mosques are wood or stone, the builders of this mosque used dried mud.

2   Two things stand out about the mosque. The first is the way it looks. The mosque's brown color makes it seem like the building just rose up from the earth around it. The second thing is the mosque's mud walls. People need to fix them very often. This makes it so the mosque's shape is always changing little by little. In fact, these repairs are a big event for the people of Djenné. Every year, people come out and help repair the mosque during the Crépissage de la Grand Mosquée festival.

3   The Great Mosque of Djenné isn't just unique; it is also very beautiful. Tourists arrive in Djenné from around the world just to see it. Some come to worship at the mosque. Others come to view a piece of art. Others yet just want to see what the largest mud building in the world looks like.

>> People are repairing the Great Mosque of Djenné. (cc by Ralf Steinberger)

≫ The Great Mosque of Djenné

Q UESTIONS

_____ 1. How often does the Crépissage de la Grand Mosquée take place?
   (A) Once a week.
   (B) Once every 10 years.
   (C) Once a month.
   (D) Once a year.

_____ 2. What is the first paragraph mainly about?
   (A) The Great Mosque of Djenné is unlike other mosques.
   (B) The Great Mosque of Djenné is made from wood and stone.
   (C) The Great Mosque of Djenné isn't unique.
   (D) The Great Mosque of Djenné was hard to build.

_____ 3. What is the main point of the second paragraph?
   (A) People don't like the mosque's color.
   (B) The mosque is special because of its looks.
   (C) The mosque was built using earth.
   (D) People think the mosque won't stand for long.

_____ 4. What is the main point of the final paragraph?
   (A) The mosque is very beautiful.
   (B) The mosque is popular with tourists.
   (C) Many people worship at the mosque.
   (D) Some people think the mosque is a piece of art.

_____ 5. What is the second thing that stands out about the Great Mosque
   of Djenné?
   (A) The mosque's color.
   (B) The mosque's shape.
   (C) The mosque's size.
   (D) The mosque's mud walls.

04 Vote for Me!

1   This school year, Annie is running for class president. A class president represents all the students in his or her grade (or "class") in a school. It is a very important job. The class president helps students with any problems and passes on their ideas to the school's leaders. The class president also helps organize events and projects for the students in his or her grade. He or she might also need to help raise money for these events and projects.

⌃ running for class president

2   Every year, the students in each grade vote for their class president. If you want to run for class president, you should make a poster about yourself and your promises. This way, students can see why they should vote for you. Here is the poster Annie made. Good luck in the election, Annie!

⌃ raising money

Vote for
Annie Wang
for 8th Grade Class President!

As your president I promise to:
1. Ask for no-uniform Fridays!
2. Start an after-school program to help students with difficult subjects!
3. Organize more school dances!
4. Listen to everyone's problems and treat everyone with respect!

Thank you for voting!

Q UESTIONS

_____1. **What is the main point of the reading?**
  (A) A class president helps organize events for the students in his or her grade.
  (B) Class president is an important role with many duties.
  (C) To be class president, you need to make a poster about yourself.
  (D) Students in each grade vote for a class president every year.

_____2. **What is the main message of the poster?**
  (A) Annie Wang wants to run for eighth grade class president this year.
  (B) If you vote for Annie, she will start a special after-school program.
  (C) Annie Wang treats everyone she meets with respect.
  (D) Annie would be a great class president, so vote for her.

_____3. **Which of the following is NOT something a class president has to do?**
  (A) Correct students' test papers.
  (B) Listen to students' problems.
  (C) Pass on students' ideas to the school's leaders.
  (D) Help raise money for student events.

_____4. **What grade is Annie in?**
  (A) Seventh grade.   (B) Ninth grade.
  (C) Eighth grade.   (D) Sixth grade.

_____5. **Here are the results of the class president election for Annie's grade. Which of the following is TRUE?**
  (A) Six students ran for class president this year in Annie's grade.
  (B) Annie got the most votes.
  (C) Annie got more votes than Terry Smith.
  (D) Greg Green got the fewest votes.

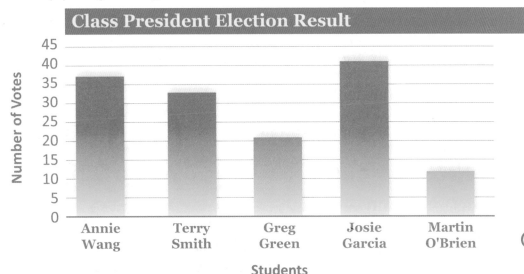

05 Healthy Mouth, Healthy Body

1   Not cleaning your teeth can lead to toothaches. But it doesn't end there. Bad oral health can also cause serious problems for your whole body!

» bacteria

2   When bacteria get into the tiny cracks in your teeth, they begin to grow in number. Soon, they start to eat away at your teeth. This makes bigger cracks where even more bacteria can grow. Before long, your teeth begin to go bad.

3   This puts the rest of your body in danger. These bad bacteria from your mouth can get into your blood. From there they travel to different parts of the body. They can get to your heart and brain and cause damage there. They can also lead to several different types of cancers.

4   Between 60 and 90 percent of school-age children have some kind of oral health problem. By ignoring this, many young people are at risk of serious health problems later in life. So brush your teeth regularly and correctly, cut down on sweet foods, and go to the dentist. These simple actions will help keep not just your mouth but also your whole body in good health!

» brushing one's teeth

⌃ toothache

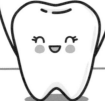

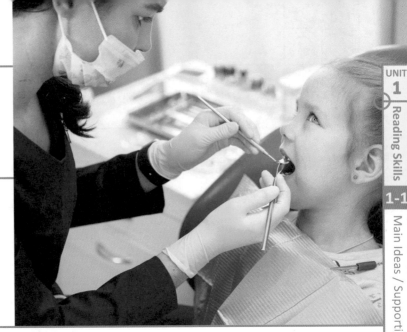

⌃ a visit to the dentist

QUESTIONS

_____1. **What is the main point of the article?**
   (A) Not cleaning your teeth can lead to toothaches.
   (B) Three simple actions can help keep your whole body in good health.
   (C) Keeping your mouth healthy is important because it affects your whole body.
   (D) It is important for young people not to ignore their oral health.

_____2. **Which of these sentences is the main message of the third paragraph?**
   (A) Bacteria from your mouth can travel and damage important parts of your body.
   (B) Young people shouldn't ignore their oral health problems if they want to be healthy in later life.
   (C) If you don't brush after eating, bacteria can grow in your mouth and eat away at your teeth.
   (D) Bacteria are dangerous because they can cause several types of cancers.

_____3. **How many school-age children have some kind of oral health problem?**
   (A) Between 60 and 90 percent.   (B) Almost 100 percent.
   (C) Below 50 percent.   (D) Between 50 and 60 percent.

_____4. **Which of the following can be damaged by bacteria from the mouth?**
   (A) Heart.   (B) Eyes.   (C) Feet.   (D) Fingers.

_____5. **Which of the following does the writer NOT suggest as a way to keep the whole body healthy?**
   (A) Brush your teeth.   (B) Eat fewer sweet foods.
   (C) Visit the dentist.   (D) Eat more salty foods.

06 Full Steam Ahead!

The Wonderful World of Steampunk Fashion

By Martin Prince | June 2021

1   Back in the 19th century, what did people think life in the 21st century would be like? Maybe they thought steam would power everything—from computers to large flying machines. What would their 19th century clothes look like with the future's "high-tech" accessories? What I'm describing is "steampunk."

2   Steampunk answers the question: What if the imagined future of 19th century people came true? Steampunk is very popular in movies and novels, but the idea also exists outside those areas. Today, artists and designers use the ideas of steampunk to create amazing designs and clothes.

Q UESTIONS

_____1. **What is the purpose of this magazine article?**
    (A) To give an answer to a difficult problem.
    (B) To point out something terrible.
    (C) To explain the history of something.
    (D) To present something interesting.

_____2. **What is the writer's tone at the beginning of the reading?**
    (A) Thoughtful.   (B) Careful.   (C) Angry.   (D) Loving.

_____3. **What is probably TRUE about Gillian Grey?**
    (A) She never wears steampunk fashion.
    (B) She doesn't know what steampunk fashion is.
    (C) She is a big fan of steampunk clothes.
    (D) She designs steampunk fashion herself.

3   "When you wear steampunk fashion you are wearing the dreams of past people," says Gillian Grey. (Grey is the owner of Full Steam Ahead—a popular steampunk fashion store.) "Therefore, steampunk fashion often gives people a strange but wonderful feeling." Each year, Grey holds a steampunk fashion show on the street outside her store. This year, seven of Gillian's favorite steampunk designers are joining the show.

4   Do you want to know what kinds of people create steampunk fashion? Do you want to know what tools and materials they use? Turn the page to find out!

_____4. **What is the writer's purpose in the fourth paragraph?**
    (A) To make you want to keep on reading.
    (B) To make you want to buy something.
    (C) To make you understand how something feels.
    (D) To make you laugh.

_____5. **Which of the following would most likely be on the next page of the magazine?**
    (A) Someone's opinion of a steampunk movie.
    (B) Interviews with steampunk clothes designers.
    (C) A short story with a steampunk setting.
    (D) Ideas on how to draw a steampunk comic.

07 Best Wishes for a Best Friend

Dear Rebecca,

1   We may not be in the same country, but I can still wish you a very happy birthday!

2   Did you think I would forget? Not a chance. Your birthday is a very special day. I remember the first time we celebrated it: the picnic, and then the rain. I was sick for weeks!

3   This year was hard, and not being able to spend time with my best friend makes it even harder. But it was the right decision to go. Family is the most important thing. And don't worry: I will be here when you get back. I just hope your grandmother gets well soon.

4   So, how are you going to celebrate today without me? Whatever you do, don't eat any ice cream with your cake. We both know how that turns out. You will definitely wake up in the middle of the night with a sore tummy. And if so, don't say I didn't warn you!

5   Have a wonderful birthday, Rebecca. You are a dear friend, and you are in my thoughts.

Love,

Jacob

PPY BIRTHDAY

QUESTIONS

_____1. What is the writer's tone in the first sentence?

(A) Sad.　　(B) Scared.　　(C) Angry.　　(D) Friendly.

_____2. What is the most likely reason Rebecca is away for her birthday?

(A) She went to visit family.

(B) She is on holiday in a foreign country.

(C) She got a new job.

(D) She is not feeling well.

_____3. What is likely TRUE about Rebecca?

(A) She doesn't like Jacob.　　(B) She loves to visit other countries.

(C) She can't eat ice cream.　　(D) She hates celebrating her birthday.

_____4. What is the writer's tone in the fourth paragraph?

(A) Serious.　　(B) Angry.　　(C) Excited.　　(D) Scared.

_____5. Which picture was likely taken the first time that Jacob and Rebecca celebrated Rebecca's birthday?

(A)

(B)

(C)

(D)

08 A Special Gift From Friendly Mart

1 James went to Friendly Mart to buy a snack this morning. When he went to pay for his snack, the cashier gave him this leaflet and two Friendly Faces.

Our customers are very important to us at Friendly Mart.
This April, we want to say a special thank you to our most loyal customers.

From April 1 to April 30,

for every NT$30 you spend in the store, you'll get a Friendly Face.
Collect Friendly Faces to get the following rewards:

10 Friendly Faces: 20% off any of the items below.

15 Friendly Faces: A cup of coffee for half price.

20 Friendly Faces: A free cup of coffee **or** 50% off any of the items below.

25 Friendly Faces: A surprise gift **or** any of the items below for free!

30 Friendly Faces: A surprise gift **and** any of the items below for free!

So for all your snacks and drinks this April, don't forget—
come to Friendly Mart!

1 ☺	2 ☺	3	4	5	Fizzy Panda Soda	Crocodile Chocolate Bar
6	7	8	9	10	Sour Power Lemon Candy	Sweet Bee Honey Cake
11	12	13	14	15	Juicee Orange Juice	Mr. Crunch Potato Chips
16	17	18	19	20	Milly's Milk Tea	Berry Burst Chewy Candy
21	22	23	24	25	King Freeze Chocolate Ice Cream	Crazy-4-Nuts Mixed Nuts
26	27	28	29	30		

Q UESTIONS

_____ 1. **What is the writer's tone at the beginning of the leaflet?**
   (A) Funny.   (B) Thankful.   (C) Excited.   (D) Loving.

_____ 2. **What is the writer's purpose in saying "So for all your snacks and drinks this April, don't forget—come to Friendly Mart!"?**
   (A) To say sorry for something bad the store did.
   (B) To stop people stealing from the store.
   (C) To make customers feel special.
   (D) To push people to buy things at the store.

_____ 3. **What is the box with numbers on the right most likely for?**
   (A) For playing a fun game.
   (B) For giving Friendly Mart a score.
   (C) For collecting Friendly Faces.
   (D) For helping you add up the cost of your items.

_____ 4. **Which of the following can you infer from the information in the leaflet?**
   (A) A Crocodile Chocolate Bar is more expensive than a Fizzy Panda Soda.
   (B) People can get the special rewards for one month only.
   (C) A bottle of Milly's Milk Tea costs the same as a cup of coffee.
   (D) The surprise gift is a Friendly Mart T-shirt.

_____ 5. **How much did James spend in the store?**
   (A) Less than NT$30.
   (B) At least NT$30 but less than NT$60.
   (C) At least NT$60 but less than NT$90.
   (D) At least NT$90 but less than NT$120.

09

A Feast Fit for a Monkey

1 If monkeys used calendars, they would always circle the last Sunday of November. On that day, the "Monkey Buffet Festival" takes place in Lopburi, Thailand. The event lets monkeys kick back and do what they love most: eat.

2 Try to picture it. Long white tables stand amid the ruins of an old temple. Someone removes the covers over the table, and you see colorful piles of fruits and vegetables. Hundreds of monkeys jump onto the tables from all around. They don't stop eating until they are too full to move.

3 It is good to be a monkey in Lopburi. The city has a thousand-year-long connection with the animal. The festival itself is more recent. A local hotel owner started it in 1989. He wanted to say "**thanks**" to the monkeys for making people want to visit Lopburi.

« The Monkey Buffet Festival attracts many tourists.

4 The Monkey Buffet Festival is not just a special day for the monkeys. Many tourists circle the day on their calendars as well. So what are you waiting for? Book a ticket and grab your camera. This is one festival you will not want to miss!

≫ Monkeys can enjoy a huge feast at the Monkey Buffet Festival.

Q UESTIONS

_____1. **What is the writer's tone in the first paragraph?**
   (A) Sad.   (B) Angry.   (C) Funny.   (D) Scared.

_____2. **What do people in Thailand probably call Lopburi?**
   (A) "Monkey City."   (B) "Hotel City."
   (C) "Fruit City."   (D) "Buffet City."

_____3. **What is the writer's purpose in the second paragraph?**
   (A) To help the reader imagine something.   (B) To make the reader laugh.
   (C) To make the reader agree with the writer.   (D) To make the reader cry.

_____4. **Why would a hotel owner in Lopburi want to say "thanks" to monkeys?**
   (A) Because they steal fruit and cause trouble.
   (B) Because they bring tourists to the city.
   (C) Because they clean up garbage around the city.
   (D) Because they keep other animals away.

_____5. **What is the writer's tone in the final paragraph?**
   (A) Careful.   (B) Heavy.   (C) Bitter.   (D) Excited.

10 Just One Song

Group: Lynne   Fey   Jerry   Tom

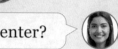 The school talent show is next week. Are we going to enter?

 We should. It will be good practice for us to play in front of an audience.

 Sounds good to me.

 Me, too. How many songs can we play?

 Just one, so we have to choose a good one. Any ideas?

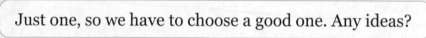 How about *Sad Sunday*? We play that one really well.

 True, but *Sad Sunday* is a bit too slow and sad.
I think we need to play something with a bit more energy.

 What about *Summer Fun*? We might need to
practice it a bit more, but it's our most fun song.

 Great idea. Everyone agree on *Summer Fun*?

 I agree.

 Hmm, I don't know.

 Why not?

 I just think *Sad Sunday* is a better song.

 But it's not right for this talent show!
Why do you always have to be so difficult, Tom?

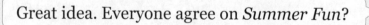

Fine, fine. *Summer Fun* it is.

 Good. So let's all meet at lunchtime tomorrow in the music room to practice. Don't forget your instruments!

 Great. See you tomorrow.

 OK.

⌄ talent show

QUESTIONS

_____ 1. **What is the purpose of this conversation?**
   (A) To ask advice about something. (B) To invite people to an event.
   (C) To learn something new. (D) To decide on something.

_____ 2. **What happens to Lynne's tone towards the end of the conversation?**
   (A) It becomes angry. (B) It becomes loving.
   (C) It becomes sad. (D) It becomes sorry.

_____ 3. **What is likely TRUE about Tom?**
   (A) He will take the day off school tomorrow. (B) He is the oldest of the four.
   (C) He often disagrees with the other three. (D) He can play guitar.

_____ 4. **What is probably TRUE about the song Summer Fun?**
   (A) It is very long. (B) It is very difficult to play.
   (C) It is fast and happy. (D) It is Fey's favorite song.

Name	Notes
Judge 1	They all have a lot of talent. What a great song! So moving. Lots of emotion.
Judge 2	The song was good, but I wanted something with more energy.
Judge 3	I think they all performed well. The singer was particularly good.

_____ 5. **Here are the judges' notes from the talent show.**
   What can we guess from these notes?
   (A) Tom left the band before the talent show.
   (B) Lynne is the singer in the band.
   (C) They changed their minds about which song to play.
   (D) One of the members' made a mistake while playing.

11
Party at My House!

To   Sarah, Winnie, Kiki, Laura

Subject   **Slumber Party at My House!**

Hi everyone,

1   Because I got good grades this semester, my mom said I could have a slumber party this weekend. She said I could invite four people, so I'm asking my four best friends to come. We can do lots of fun things, like watch movies, eat snacks, and stay up all night talking!

2   The party will begin at 6 p.m. on Saturday. Mom said she doesn't want to cook for so many people. So we can order pizza from the new pizza restaurant near our house!

3   I want everyone to have a great time, so let me know what you want to do. It can be anything you want. That way we can all have fun.

4   Mom also said she would take us out for breakfast the next morning. So tell your parents you'll be home around midday on Sunday.

5   OK! Let me know by Wednesday if you can come. That way I have enough time to prepare.

6   Can't wait to hang out with you all! It's going to be **so** much fun!

Molly

Send

QUESTIONS

_____1. **Why is Molly's mother letting her have a slumber party?**
   (A) Because she is ordering pizza on Saturday night.
   (B) Because she is taking Molly's friends to breakfast on Sunday.
   (C) Because Molly wants to stay up late talking with her friends.
   (D) Because Molly got good grades this semester.

_____2. **Why will the girls order pizza for dinner?**
   (A) Because pizza is Molly's favorite food.
   (B) Because Molly's mother doesn't want to cook.
   (C) Because they can do anything they want.
   (D) Because a new pizza restaurant opened near Molly's house.

_____3. **How does Molly create interest in the first paragraph?**
   (A) By listing examples.   (B) By asking a difficult question.
   (C) By making her friends laugh. (D) By telling a sad story.

_____4. **What does the word "so" do in the phrase "It's going to be so much fun!"?**
   (A) It introduces a result.   (B) It expresses agreement.
   (C) It introduces a next step. (D) It emphasizes something.

_____5. **Here is Sarah's reply to Molly's email.**

To:	Molly
Subject:	**RE: Slumber Party at my House!**

Hi Molly! Thanks for the invitation! I can definitely come. I have my piano class on Saturday evening, so I will be a little late. But I can be at your place at 7 p.m. Please save me some pizza! Could we also play some board games? I can bring some of my own over if you don't have any. Let me know! See you on Saturday! Can't wait!

Sarah

Sarah has a piano class on Saturday. What is the effect of this?
(A) She won't be able to go to Molly's slumber party.
(B) She will have to leave Molly's house early.
(C) She will not arrive at Molly's house on time.
(D) She won't be able to eat any pizza.

12

A Hunter That Dreams in Green

1 When we hear the word "hunter," we usually think of animals. But did you know that there are plant hunters, too?

2 Plant hunters hunt down hard-to-find plants. It is a lot harder than it sounds. These plants might be on the highest mountains, or in the deepest caves. So you need some unique skills to do this job.

3 For example, a plant hunter must be able to live in the wild for days, even weeks. They must be able to climb tall trees and reach difficult places. But most of all, they must know their plants.

4 Hung Hsin-chieh has all these skills. Hung never graduated high school, and he taught himself how to hunt plants. Yet he is still one of Taiwan's best plant hunters. All it takes is drive, hard work, and a love of the wild.

5 Plant hunters can help scientists find and study rare plants. They can also track the many types of plants we lose for good every year. Sadly, since many plants are disappearing around the world, their work is now more important than ever.

« Plant hunters help track the plants we lose for good.

≫ Hung Hsin-chieh hunting plants
(Source: https://www.facebook.com/photo.php?fbid=3749780738442446&set=pb.100002316707210.-2207520000..&type=3)

QUESTIONS

_____1. **Why are plant hunters more important than ever?**
   (A) There are not many plant hunters anymore.
   (B) Plants are disappearing around the world. ·
   (C) Plant hunters can climb trees.
   (D) Scientists need plant hunters to study plants.

_____2. **Which is an effect of many plants being in hard-to-reach places?**
   (A) Plant hunters need to be able to climb.
   (B) Plant hunters are used by scientists.
   (C) Plant hunters need to study at school.
   (D) Plant hunters must love plants.

_____3. **How does the writer get the reader's attention in the final sentence?**
   (A) By making the reader think about the past.
   (B) By giving the reader an example.
   (C) By making the reader laugh.
   (D) By making the reader feel something.

_____4. **Which of the following does the writer do in the third paragraph?**
   (A) Gives an opinion.　　　　(B) Tells a joke.
   (C) Tells a story.　　　　(D) Describes a job.

_____5. **How does the writer get the reader's attention in the first paragraph?**
   (A) By giving a large number.　　(B) By telling a story.
   (C) By asking a question.　　　(D) By telling a joke.

» cleaning the beach

Keeping the Coast Clean

Clean-Up at White Sand Beach

Details	**Event by:** Maggie Wang
	📍 White Sand Beach
	🕐 Monday, June 3 from 8 a.m. to 11 a.m.
	👥 15 people are currently going.

1 Come and help us keep White Sand Beach clean! White Sand Beach is a wonderful place. People love to relax or play beach games on the sand. And it is a very popular place for children to run around and play. However, there is currently a lot of trash on the beach. There are bottles, plastic bags, paper cups, and candy wrappers. We want the beach to be a clean, safe place for everyone to enjoy. So we are looking for volunteers to come and help us pick up the trash on the beach.

2 We will provide you with trash bags and gloves. We will also provide snacks and drinks. All you need to bring is yourself and a helpful attitude (and maybe a hat, as it will be a sunny day)!

3 We will meet outside the beach café at 8 a.m. We look forward to seeing you there!

Q UESTIONS

_____1. **Which of the following is the reading?**
  (A) A news article. (B) An invite.
  (C) An interview. (D) A song.

_____2. **Which of these begins the reading?**
  (A) A funny story. (B) A surprising fact.
  (C) Important information. (D) A wish.

_____3. **Why is the event in the reading happening?**
  (A) There is a lot of trash on the beach.
  (B) People love to relax on the beach.
  (C) Monday, June 3 will be very sunny.
  (D) Fifteen people are currently going.

_____4. **How does the writer end the second paragraph?**
  (A) With a play on words. (B) With a sad story.
  (C) With a piece of advice. (D) With an example.

Date: June 4

Subject: **A Big Thank You!**

To everyone who joined us at White Sand Beach yesterday,

Thank you so much for all your help. Everyone did such a wonderful job. The local people were all very happy! We also want to say a special thank you to Matt Green. He collected the most trash on the day—32 kilograms! We just posted details of our next beach clean-up at Blue Sea Beach. It would be great to see you all again there.

Thank you all again!

_____5. **Matt attended the event on June 3. On June 4, he got this email. Why did Matt get a special thank you in the email?**
  (A) He collected the most trash.
  (B) He made the local people very happy.
  (C) He signed up for the clean-up at Blue Sea Beach.
  (D) He showed up to the clean-up at White Sand Beach.

« online shopping

Push, Push, Buy!

⌃ star ratings and reviews

1   You are doing some shopping online and suddenly a message appears next to the picture of a coffee machine. "Only 1 left!" it says. Wow, you think. It must be good if it is so popular. Should you buy it? You don't really drink much coffee . . . . While you are thinking, another message pops up. "Twenty other people are currently looking at this item." You'd better buy it fast before someone else does! Quickly, you click the "Buy Now!" button.

2   Buying something without planning is called "impulse buying." It is a real problem for a lot of shoppers. People spend a lot of money on things they never use. Shopping websites use many clever tricks to encourage impulse buying. These **include** sales, bestseller tags, star ratings and reviews, and timers.

3   To stop yourself being pushed into impulse buying, ask yourself a few questions before you click "Buy." Do I really need this item? What would I use it for? What else could I buy for this amount of money? Remember, online stores want your money, and they will try anything to get you to spend it!

» sales sign

QUESTIONS

_____1. **How does the writer create interest in the first paragraph?**
(A) By asking difficult questions.
(B) By telling a common story.
(C) By describing something beautiful.
(D) By giving some wonderful facts.

_____2. **How does the writer end the reading?**
(A) With a joke.　(B) With a personal story.
(C) With an example.　(D) With a message to be careful.

_____3. **What is the effect of buying things without planning?**
(A) People give the things they buy lots of good reviews.
(B) People spend a lot of money on things they never use.
(C) People work harder to make more money.
(D) People ask themselves questions while shopping.

_____4. **Why does the writer use the word "include" in the second paragraph?**
(A) To introduce a list of examples.
(B) To introduce the writer's opinion.
(C) To introduce a story.
(D) To introduce a serious thought.

_____5. **Here is how much Jenny spends each month on online shopping. In March, she began to ask herself "Do I really need this?" before buying an item. How did Jenny's spending change as a result?**

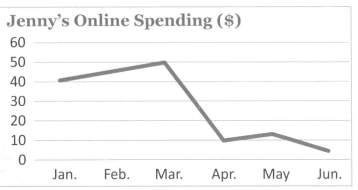

Jenny's Online Spending ($)

(A) It went up a little.　(B) It went down a lot.
(C) It dropped to zero.　(D) It doubled.

Good News for the Planet

⌃ plastic pollution

» plastic bags

Tina: And for our last story of the evening, some good news for the planet. Plastic bags take over 150 years to disappear naturally. As a result, they pollute our land and our oceans. However, several planet-friendly alternatives are making
5   their way onto the market. Our environment reporter James Marley has the story. Over to you, James.

James: Thank you, Tina. I have in my hand here a common, cheap plastic bag—or do I? It looks like a plastic bag. It feels like a plastic bag. But in fact it isn't made of plastic. It is made
10   from 100% biodegradable materials. When you're finished using it, just put it in a cup and add hot water. **Then** watch it disappear! After it's gone, you can pour it down the sink. It leaves no toxic waste, just CO_2 and water. If these new bags become popular, it will mean the end of
15   plastic bags in our oceans. Back to you, Tina.

Tina: Thank you, James. That's all we have time for today . . . .

❶ Products can be used, reused and recycled.

❷ degradation triggered by heat, UV light and/or mechanical stress

❸ H2O, CO2 & biomass

❹ photosynthesis

❺ trees and plants

QUESTIONS

_____1. **Which of the following is the reading?**
  (A) A talk between two friends.
  (B) A person's opinion.
  (C) A news report.
  (D) A set of questions and answers.

_____2. **How does James create interest in his first few sentences?**
  (A) By giving his ideas.
  (B) By saying something surprising.
  (C) By telling a story.
  (D) By giving a famous example.

_____3. **In James's speech, what does the word "Then" show?**
  (A) A step will follow.
  (B) A question will follow.
  (C) A joke will follow.
  (D) An opinion will follow.

_____4. **Why do plastic bags pollute our land and oceans?**
  (A) They take a long time to disappear naturally.
  (B) They are cheap to buy.
  (C) People use them once and then throw them away.
  (D) They are used a lot all over the world.

_____5. **Which of the following sentences from the reading shows a cause-and-effect relationship?**
  (A) "And for our final story of the evening, some good news for the planet."
  (B) "However, several planet-friendly alternatives are making their way onto the market."
  (C) "If these new bags become popular, it will mean the end of plastic bags in our oceans."
  (D) "After it's gone, you can pour it down the sink."

>> older adults

16 A Question for the Class

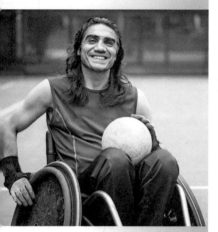

⌃ disabled person

⌃ pregnant woman

A teacher asked her students a question. Here's how they responded:

Julia: I often see young children using them. I don't think they should because they are young and have a lot of energy. I think only old people, disabled people, and pregnant women should be able to use them.

Mark: I think they should be available for anyone who needs them. I often feel sick on buses and trains and need to sit down. Once I was really ill and one was empty. But I didn't sit because I thought people would shout at me.

Kim: I disagree with Mark. If you said anyone could use them, then people would take advantage of the system. For example, people could give silly excuses like "I need to sit because I have a heavy bag." I think the system is fine the way it is.

Gregg: I think we should get rid of them altogether. Most people are kind. They would always give up a seat if they saw that someone needed it. Having them just puts pressure on people.

Q UESTIONS

_____1. **What question did the teacher most likely ask her students?**

(A) "Who should be able to use buses and trains?"

(B) "Should buses and trains cost less for some people and more for others?"

(C) "Should buses and trains be free for everyone?"

(D) "Who should the priority seats on buses and trains be for?"

_____2. **Which of the following sentences from the reading shows a cause-and-effect relationship?**

(A) "If you said anyone could use them, then people would take advantage of the system."

(B) "Only old people, disabled people, and pregnant women should be able to use them."

(C) "I think they should be available for anyone who needs them."

(D) "I don't think they should because they are young and have a lot of energy."

_____3. **Which of the following is TRUE about Mark?**

(A) His mother is going to have a baby soon.

(B) He usually walks to school.

(C) He often feels sick when taking the train.

(D) He often shouts at people on the bus.

_____4. **What tone do the students use to respond to the teacher's question?**

(A) Funny.   (B) Serious.   (C) Loving.   (D) Shy.

_____5. **After the discussion, the teacher asked the class to vote on who they agreed with. Here are the results of the vote. Which of the following is NOT true?**

(A) More students agreed with Gregg than with Mark.

(B) Kim got more votes than anyone else.

(C) More than half the class agreed with Kim.

(D) More people agreed with Julia than with Gregg and Mark together.

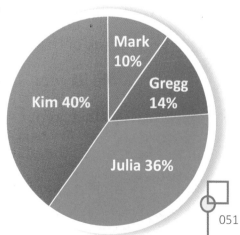

Mark 10%

Gregg 14%

Kim 40%

Julia 36%

17 Which News Can We Trust?

1   Media used to be simple. If you wanted the news, you bought a newspaper. You didn't have a lot of choices: maybe two or three to pick from. And these newspapers paid journalists to go out and find the news. If they wrote lies, those people would lose their jobs.

2   The Internet changed all that. Now there are thousands of news websites to choose from, and a lot of them are free. This means they cannot pay journalists. So how do they get their news? Maybe they get the information secondhand, from newspapers or other websites. Or maybe they just make it all up.

3   "Fake news" is news with inaccurate information. Sometimes this is on purpose. Sometimes it is because of a simple mistake. But fake news is a huge problem. It can even be hard to know what is real and what is not sometimes.

4   How can a reader spot fake news? Always think of the reputation of the website. Media companies and journalists care about their reputations. They might not be right all the time, but they won't try to trick their readers on purpose.

» journalist

newspaper vs. online news

Q UESTIONS

_____1. **Why was it easier to trust news in the past?**
   (A) Paid journalists wrote about the news.
   (B) There were many newspapers to pick from.
   (C) All information was secondhand.
   (D) People did not make up the news.

_____2. **How does the writer create interest in the first and second paragraphs?**
   (A) By giving the reader lots of facts and large numbers.
   (B) By showing how things are different now compared to before.
   (C) By asking many questions one after another.
   (D) By showing how two different things are actually very similar.

_____3. **What is the writer's purpose in the final paragraph?**
   (A) To make the reader laugh.   (B) To tell the reader a sad story.
   (C) To make the reader angry.   (D) To teach the reader something.

_____4. **Which of the following news stories is least likely to be fake news?**
   (A) A story from a free website, with no writer.
   (B) A story from a website you never heard of.
   (C) A story with many words spelled wrong.
   (D) A story from a major newspaper in your city.

_____5. **What is the main idea of the second paragraph?**
   (A) Newspapers are less important now.
   (B) Some websites just make up the news.
   (C) The Internet changed media.
   (D) There are now thousands of news websites.

≫ fake news

≫ news media
   outlets

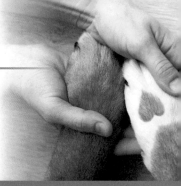

18 Our Animals Need You!

Our Animals Need You!

1   Do you love animals? Are you over the age of 18? Do you have at least three hours of free time a week?

2   At the **Safe Home Animals Shelter** we are looking for helpers.

3   We currently house over fifty dogs and cats, and they need lots of care and attention. We need people to help with different jobs around the shelter. These include:

>> **Feeding our animals**

>> **Keeping our shelter clean**

>> **Walking the dogs**

>> **Playing with the cats**

>> **Giving some of the animals medicine**

>> **Posting about our animals on social media**

4   **Please note:**

Our shelter does not make any money, so we are not able to pay our helpers. But we can promise that the work is very rewarding. In return for your help, you will get lots of love from our wonderful animals.

5   If you think this is something you would like to do, please call us on 555-345-234 and leave your information. We will call you back if we think you would be good as one of our helpers.

Q UESTIONS

_____1. **How does the writer catch the reader's attention in the reading?**
   (A) By telling sad stories.   (B) By speaking directly to the reader.
   (C) By making jokes.   (D) By using lots of describing words.

_____2. **What is the main point of the reading?**
   (A) The Safe Home Animal Shelter is looking for people to help them.
   (B) If you want to help, you should call 555-345-234.
   (C) The Safe Home Animal Shelter takes care of over fifty dogs and cats.
   (D) The Safe Home Animal Shelter needs people to help walk their dogs.

_____3. **Which of the following things will helpers NOT need to do?**
   (A) Clean the shelter.   (B) Give food to the animals.
   (D) Help catch street animals.   (C) Play with some of the animals.

_____4. **Which sentence from the reading shows a cause-and-effect relationship?**
   (A) "We currently house over fifty dogs and cats, and they need lots of care and attention."
   (B) "Our shelter does not make any money, so we are not able to pay our helpers."
   (C) "Do you have at least three hours of free time a week?"
   (D) "We need people to help with different tasks around the shelter."

_____5. **Four people called the Safe Home Animal Shelter to offer to help. Which person/people would not get a call back from the shelter?**
   (A) Helen.   (B) Kevin and Mavis.
   (C) Jack and Mavis.   (D) Helen, Kevin, and Jack.

Name	Age	Free Time Per Week
Jack	17	1 hour on Mondays, 2 hours on Fridays.
Mavis	25	1 hour on Wednesdays, 1 hour on Saturdays.
Helen	19	4 hours on Saturdays.
Kevin	32	2 hours on Saturdays, 2 hours on Sundays.

19 Fighting for Girls to Stay in School

In the world's poorest countries, many girls do not get to go to school. One former world leader is trying to change that.

By Lisa Strong

⌃ Julia Gillard, Chair of the Board of Directors of the Global Partnership for Education (cc by DFID - UK Department for International Development)

1   Julia Gillard used to be the leader of Australia. Now she leads the Global Partnership for Education (GPE). The organization helps raise money to support education in around 70 of the world's poorest countries. One of the GPE's main efforts in these countries is to increase the number of girls in schools.

2   According to Gillard, many poor families face "very tough choices" when it comes to educating their children. Many only have enough money to send one of their children to school. And the girls must often stay at home to work for their families. They never get a chance to make a better life for themselves.

3   But helping girls go to school is not just good for the girls themselves. Gillard believes a country can become richer, safer, and more peaceful "if girls are in school and learning."

Read on to learn about some of GPE's success stories . . . .

˅ girls in poor countries going to school (cc by Global Partnership for Education)

˅ girls in poor countries staying at home and working

Q UESTIONS

_____ 1. **What is the effect if girls go to school?**

(A) Their countries become less safe.

(B) Their families become poorer.

(C) Their countries become richer.

(D) Their lives become harder.

_____ 2. **Which of the following is one of the main aims of the GPE?**

(A) To get more girls in schools in the world's poorest countries.

(B) To make sure people in poor countries have modern medicine.

(C) To stop people in poor countries hunting animals for money.

(D) To help when bad weather affects poor countries.

_____ 3. **What tone does the writer use in the second paragraph "According to Gillard, . . ."?**

(A) Funny.　(B) Excited.　(C) Afraid.　(D) Sad.

_____ 4. **How does the writer interest the reader in the subheading "In the world's poorest countries, . . ."?**

(A) By telling a funny story.

(B) By giving a surprising number.

(C) By giving a serious fact.

(D) By using beautiful language.

_____ 5. **Which of these will you probably find in the next part of the reading?**

(A) A list of the world's 70 poorest countries.

(B) A happy story about girls in school in a poor country.

(C) A story about Julia Gillard when she was a little girl.

(D) A sad story about a poor family.

UNIT 1 🎧 20

20 Stand Up and Say Something

⌃ sexual harassment

Dear diary,

1   What a day; I don't even know where to begin.

2   I was on the bus, like any other afternoon. It was very crowded. All of a sudden, the man next to me started bumping into me. I even felt his hand touching my behind. This was no accident. That man was taking advantage of me.

3   At first, I couldn't move. I felt shocked and scared. But then another feeling arrived: anger. I turned around and faced the man. I looked him in the eye and shouted: "hands off, pervert!" He was so surprised. He never expected his victim to stand up for herself.

4   This terrible experience will stay with me for a long time. But it is not all bad. Some good came from it as well. Other people really wanted to help me. One woman even walked me all the way home. And the pervert didn't get away. He is now with the police.

5   I am glad that I didn't let him get away with it, and I feel proud of myself. I think it is important to speak out. It may be difficult, but at least you will not be alone.

≫ Say no to sexual harassment.   ≫ "no sexual harassment" sign on bus

QUESTIONS

_____ 1. **What happened after the writer spoke out on the bus?**
  (A) The bus became crowded.   (B) The pervert didn't get away.
  (C) The pervert was angry.   (D) The writer was scared.

_____ 2. **What could this article best be described as?**
  (A) A story.   (B) A news article.
  (C) A piece of advice.   (D) A list of events.

_____ 3. **What is the writer's tone in this article?**
  (A) Funny.   (B) Careful.   (C) Serious.   (D) Excited.

_____ 4. **What is the writer trying to say in the final paragraph?**
  (A) Don't ride the bus.   (B) If someone hurts you, say something.
  (C) We all feel alone sometimes. (D) Bad people hurt others every day.

_____ 5. **Which picture was likely taken right after the writer got off the bus?**
  (A)   (B)

  (C)   (D)

UNIT
2

Word Study

Synonyms / Antonyms / Words In Context

In this unit, you will practice identifying words with the same or opposite meanings, and guessing the meanings of words from their context. These skills will help you understand new vocabulary and build vocabulary on your own in the future.

Don't Ignore Us

Life in the Modern World

Cherry Chen

1   Last year, I visited Los Angeles in the United
States. I couldn't believe how many homeless people
there were. I looked online and saw there were over 40,000
homeless people in LA! In Taipei, I **hardly ever** see any
homeless people. It is not a problem in Taiwan, I thought.

⌃ homeless people in Taipei

2   Then last weekend I visited the shopping mall in Taipei Main Station. There were many people—mostly old—sleeping on the street outside. I was shocked. I did some research and found there were around 650 homeless people in Taipei. Of course, that's a lot fewer than in LA, but still, they exist.

3   I was curious, so I bought a lunchbox and gave it to one of the men. I started chatting with him to find out his story. He was 57 years old. He never married and has no children. He used to work in a factory, but he lost his job five years ago and couldn't find another one. He will get money from the government only when he turns 65. I asked what people could do to help homeless people in Taiwan. He said, "Don't ignore us."

Q UESTIONS

_____1. **What is the opposite of "hardly ever"?**
    (A) Never.   (B) Very rarely.   (C) Finally.   (D) Almost always.

_____2. **Which of these words could the writer use in place of "shocked"?**
    (A) Excited.   (B) Surprised.   (C) Bored.   (D) Tired.

_____3. **What does "one" mean in the reading?**
    (A) Job.   (B) Child.   (C) Factory.   (D) Money.

_____4. **What does the word "turn" mean in reading?**
    (A) Change shape.   (B) Move in a circle.
    (C) Reach an age.   (D) Go bad.

_____5. **What does "us" mean in the final sentence?**
    (A) The people of Taipei.   (B) Homeless people in Taiwan.
    (C) People under 65.   (D) Factory workers.

22

>> African mask

An Important Part of African Culture

Becoming the Spirits:
My Journey into the World of African Masks

▌ *Preface* ▌

1　　I saw my first African mask when I was thirteen on a school trip to a museum. **It** was red and gold, with big empty eyes and a long chin. For many months, I couldn't stop thinking about that face. It was as if it had a spell on me. So I decided to learn all I could about African masks.

2　　Over many years, I read every book I could find on the subject. I learned that masks play an important part in the ceremonies of many African tribes. They represent many things—spirits of the dead, animals, or heroes from **myths and legends**. When a person puts on a mask, he or she stops being human and *becomes* the spirit of the mask.

3　　The more I learned, the more I wanted to know. But to truly understand the secrets of these masks, I knew I had to visit Africa myself and meet the makers of these masks in person. I had to **see** people using them **with my own eyes**. This book is the story of that journey and what I **found out**.

≪ African tribespeople in masks

Q UESTIONS

_____1. **What does "It" mean in the second sentence?**
(A) The African mask in the museum.
(B) The museum itself.
(C) The school trip to the museum.
(D) The book *Becoming the Spirits*.

_____2. **What are "myths and legends"?**
(A) Types of plans.   (B) Delicious foods.
(C) Old stories.   (D) Pieces of music.

_____3. **What is another word for "found out"?**
(A) Lost.   (B) Traveled.   (C) Chose.   (D) Discovered.

_____4. **What does the phrase "to see something with one's own eyes" mean?**
(A) To see something on TV.   (B) To see something in the dark.
(C) To see something from far away.   (D) To see something in real life.

_____5. **Some people read *Becoming the Spirits* and wrote reviews of it online. Here is one of those reviews.**

> **Katie Chu**   ★ ★ ★ ★ ★
>
> "What a **fascinating** topic! I learned so much! I especially loved the section about the masks of the Yoruba people. Thank you for writing this book!"

Which of these is the opposite of "fascinating"?
(A) Difficult.   (B) Boring.   (C) Dangerous.   (D) Strange.

23

» Shops and restaurants are closed due to COVID-19.

⌃ COVID-19

⌃ SORRY due to COVID-19 we are CLOSED

Life in Lockdown

It's December 2020. Richard from the UK is making a video call to his friend Lin from Taiwan.

Richard

Lin

Richard: Hi, Lin! Wow, it's so good to see you!

Lin: Hi, Richard! You too! How is the COVID-19 situation with you?

5 **Richard:** Well, we're in lockdown here. So I can't meet any of my friends. And almost all shops and restaurants are closed. But I'm not sick. So at least **that**'s a positive.

Lin: I'm glad to hear you're healthy. How are your parents?

Richard: Dad's fine. Mom started coughing yesterday so she's

10 **quarantining** in her bedroom. She can't come out. She's getting a test soon, so we'll know if she has the virus or not.

Lin: I hope she's OK. How are you getting food if all the shops are closed?

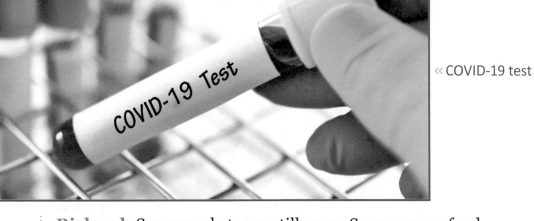

« COVID-19 test

Richard: Supermarkets are still open. So we can go food

shopping if we need to. But we must wear masks and stay

15   far away from people when we're in there.

Lin: It sounds like a really **tough** time. I hope things

improve there soon.

Richard: Me, too. Hey, let's talk about something less

miserable. How's your new cat?

20 **Lin:** She's great! Let me call her over—Molly! Here, Molly!

 **UESTIONS**

_____ 1. **What does the word "that" mean in the sentence "So at least that's a positive"?**

    (A) Richard not being sick.   (B) Richard not being able to meet his friends.

    (C) Richard talking to Lin.   (D) Shops and restaurants being closed.

_____ 2. **If someone is "quarantining," what are they doing?**

    (A) Cooking lots of food.   (B) Having a party with lots of people.

    (C) Going out shopping.   (D) Staying away from other people.

_____ 3. **What is another word for "tough"?**

    (A) Funny.   (B) Blind.   (C) Careful.   (D) Difficult.

_____ 4. **What does "improve" most likely mean?**

    (A) Get better.   (B) Slow down.

    (C) Make money.   (D) Make bigger.

_____ 5. **What is the opposite of "miserable"?**

    (A) Poor.   (B) Happy.   (C) Sick.   (D) Simple.

24 A Chance to Visit France

NOTICE

Student Exchange Program

December 1, 2021

1   Next March-April, students from grade 7 will be able to **participate** in a student exchange program. From March 7 to March 14, students from Collège Paul Lapie in France will be visiting our school. And from March 28 to April 4 students from our school will be visiting Collège Paul Lapie. This is a wonderful chance to meet people from another culture and practice your French with **native speakers**.

2   During their visit, the French students will stay at the homes of our students. And during their visit to France, our students will stay with the French students' families.

3   If you want to sign up for this program, please **do so** with Ms. Janvier before December 14. There are only 15 places available for this program, so sign up quickly to avoid being **disappointed**. But remember, you must ask your parents' **permission** first!

Thank you,

Mr. Quill

Head of Modern Languages

˅ meeting people from other cultures

⌃ signing up

QUESTIONS

_____ 1. **What is another word for "participate"?**

(A) Take.　　(B) Fix.　　(C) Move.　　(D) Join.

_____ 2. **Who does the writer mean by "native speakers"?**

(A) Mr. Quill and Ms. Janvier.

(B) Students from Collège Paul Lapie, France.

(C) Students from grade 7.

(D) The students' parents.

_____ 3. **What does the phrase "do so" mean in the reading?**

(A) Visit a school in France.　　(B) Practice your language skills.

(C) Sign up for the program.　　(D) Meet people from a different culture.

_____ 4. **Which of these people is the opposite of "disappointed"?**

(A)　　　　　(B)　　　　　(C)　　　　　(D)

_____ 5. **What do you do if you ask someone's "permission"?**

(A) Ask them if it is OK to do something.

(B) Ask them for money.

(C) Ask their name and phone number.

(D) Ask them if they have any plans later.

25 Stop Those Ums and Ahs

1   When we speak, we often use words and phrases like "um," "ah," "like," and "you know." They don't mean anything, but they help keep a **conversation** going. If you are preparing to speak to an audience, however, you should try to get rid of these words from your speech.

2   There are two important reasons why you should do this. Firstly, when you are speaking in public, you usually want to express an important message. Filling your speech with **empty words** will make your message sound less **powerful**. Secondly, these words can be very distracting. If your audience realizes you keep using such words, they will stop paying attention to your message. Instead, they will spend their time listening for the next "like" or "um" you will say.

3   In order to break this habit, you can practice slowing down your speech. Our mouths often work faster than our minds. So we use words like "um" while our minds catch up. When you are speaking in public, **take your time** and try not to be nervous. Your speech will flow much better, and your audience will hear your message loud and clear.

« speaking in public

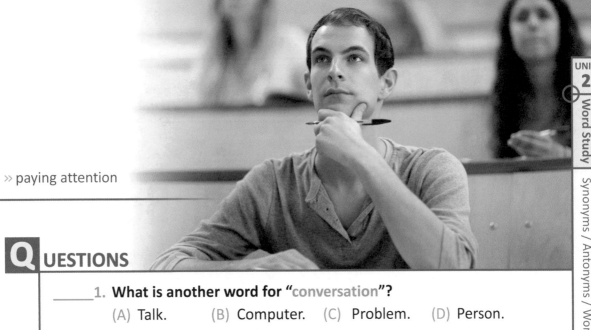

>> paying attention

QUESTIONS

_____ 1. **What is another word for "conversation"?**

(A) Talk.　　(B) Computer.　(C) Problem.　(D) Person.

_____ 2. **What is the opposite of "powerful"?**

(A) Strong.　(B) Loud.　　(C) Difficult.　(D) Weak.

_____ 3. **What does the writer mean by "empty words"?**

(A) Words with difficult spelling.

(B) Words with no meaning.

(C) Words nobody understands.

(D) Words in a foreign language.

_____ 4. **What does the writer mean by "take your time"?**

(A) Do not hurry.　　　　(B) Use words like "um" and "ah."

(C) Speak more loudly.　　(D) Do not stop.

_____ 5. **You can learn more about how to speak in public on the website below.**

https://www.teachme.com.tw/courses/publicspeaking

Public Speaking Online Course

Preparing for Your Speech

>> **Lesson 2:** Planning Your Speech

>> **Lesson 3:** Using Your Voice

>> **Lesson 4:** Body Language

>> **Lesson 5:** Staying **Calm**

What is the opposite of "calm"?

(A) Happy.　　(B) Tired.　　(C) Nervous.　　(D) Lonely.

26 A Place for Bees

Community Notice

Help Our Local Bees!

1 Did you know that most bees don't live in a hive with thousands of other bees? That's right. Nine out of ten bees actually live **alone**. They don't make honey, and they rarely attack people (because they have no hive to protect!). As a result, they are **no danger** to pets or humans. Bees also help pollinate important food plants. Without them, lots of our food would not grow.

2 Sadly, these bees are disappearing. Like many of us, these bees like to have their own private little rooms. They love to live in long, thin holes, like the **ones** in bamboo sticks. Our clean, modern buildings and tidy gardens don't provide many places for them to live.

3 But we can help! Making a special bee hotel is easy. You just need a few simple materials and **basic** tools. If you would like to build a bee hotel, come and see me at 4 Oak Road. I have everything you'll need. And I will show you how to build **one**!

4 Thank you for helping our local bees!

John Smith

« Bees live in long, thin holes.

⌃ Bees help pollinate food plants.

QUESTIONS

_____1. **What does "alone" in the first paragraph most likely mean?**
   (A) With friends.
   (B) Without food.
   (C) Without others.
   (D) With lots of money.

_____2. **What is another word for "no danger"?**
   (A) Foreign.
   (B) Delicious.
   (C) Mean.
   (D) Safe.

_____3. **What does "ones" in the second paragraph refer to?**
   (A) Modern buildings.
   (B) Long, thin holes.
   (C) Tidy Gardens.
   (D) Private rooms.

_____4. **What is the opposite of "basic" in the third paragraph?**
   (A) Special.
   (B) Easy.
   (C) Cheap.
   (D) Colorful.

_____5. **What is "one" in the third paragraph?**
   (A) A tool.
   (B) Jill's house.
   (C) A bee.
   (D) A bee hotel.

27 The Dogs With the Hardest Jobs

1 Dogs make great pets. But they are also good **learners**. Therefore, we often train them to help us work. Some of the hardest-working dogs are police dogs. These dogs have many important duties. They search for drugs and bombs. They help find missing people. And they protect police officers from attackers.

⌃ Belgian Malonois

2 Many **breeds** of dogs make great police dogs. But currently the most popular is the Belgian Malonois. The Malonois is a medium-sized dog with a long, strong body. It is also very fast and has lots of energy and focus. As a result, it is **perfect** for difficult police work.

« police dog

⌃ training a police dog

⌃ Police dogs help search for drugs and bombs.

3 Police-dog training is hard and takes a long time. By the end, the dogs must be able to obey their masters without pause. After training, police dogs might work for up to nine years before they can retire. When they do, they often go and live with their old masters. In some countries, they get money from the government each year to help pay for their care. We really owe these hard-working dogs a lot. So it is important we treat them well during their senior years!

QUESTIONS

_____ 1. **What is another word for "learners"?**
   (A) Owners.　(B) Runners.　(C) Students.　(D) Animals.

_____ 2. **Which of these means the same as "breeds"?**
   (A) Types.　(B) Stories.　(C) Pieces.　(D) Colors.

_____ 3. **What is the opposite of "perfect"?**
   (A) Beautiful.　(B) Terrible.　(C) Large.　(D) Correct.

_____ 4. **Which of these is another way to say "senior years"?**
   (A) Dinner time.　　(B) Summer break.
   (C) Night time.　　(D) Old age.

_____ 5. **If someone "retires," what do they stop doing?**
   (A) Reading.　(B) Working.　(C) Learning.　(D) Crying.

28 The Tree of Love

1   In a forest in Germany, there is a 500-year-old oak tree with a hole in its **trunk**. Inside the hole, there are letters from people all over the world.

2   People call it the Bridegroom's Oak. In the 19th century, two local youngsters, Minna Ohrt and Wilhelm Schütte-Felsche were deeply in love. But Minna's parents would not let them marry. So the two wrote letters to each other in secret. They used an oak tree in the forest as a hiding place for these letters. **Finally**, Minna's father gave in and let them get married. And they **tied the knot** under their special tree on June 2, 1891.

« Bridegroom's Oak
(cc by Armin von Werner)

⌄ People send letters to the Bridegroom's Oak.
(cc by Holger.Ellgaard)

3   After the story of **the happy couple** spread, people began sending letters to the tree. These letter-writers hoped someone would find their letters, read them, and write back. They hoped they might find true love this way. In 1927, the local mail service **set up** a ladder by the tree. And a mailman began to officially deliver letters there. Still today, letters regularly arrive at the Bridegroom's Oak from people looking to find love.

Q UESTIONS

_____1. **Each of the following pictures shows a "trunk." Which meaning of the word does the writer use in the first sentence?**

(A) (B) (C) (D)

_____2. **Which of these means the same as "finally"?**
(A) In the beginning. (B) In the end.
(C) In the future. (D) In the past.

_____3. **What does the phrase "tied the knot" most likely mean?**
(A) Stopped fighting. (B) Got married.
(C) Climbed a tree. (D) Wrote a letter.

_____4. **Who does the writer mean by "the happy couple"?**
(A) Workers from the local mail service.
(B) People from all over the world.
(C) Minna Ohrt and Wilhelm Schütte-Felsche.
(D) Minna Ohrt's parents.

_____5. **What is the opposite of "set up"?**
(A) Took down. (B) Gave away. (C) Put on. (D) Let go.

29 A Busy Work Week

Jim is a firefighter. Here is a page from his diary.

1 Mar. 12

A quiet day today. In the morning we got a call because a cat got **stuck** up a tree and couldn't get down. The cat was nervous and tried to scratch me. Thank goodness for my thick gloves!

⌃ being scratched by a cat

2 Mar. 14

There was a fire in an old house today. The mother was cooking with oil and it caught fire. We put out the fire, but there was a lot of damage. Luckily, the family **escaped** from the burning house quickly and no one was hurt.

« firefighter

QUESTIONS

_____ 1. **If something is "stuck," what can't it do?**
(A) Make a sound. (B) Breathe.
(C) See. (D) Move.

_____ 2. **What does the word "escape" most likely mean?**
(A) Run away from something dangerous.
(B) Call for help when something bad happens.
(C) Take a break from a difficult job.
(D) Teach important information.

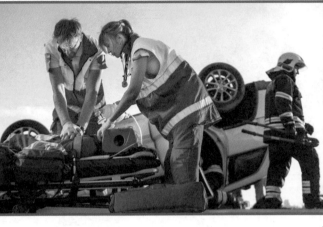
⌃ car crash

⌃ putting out a fire

3 **Mar. 16**

A sad day today. There was a big car crash on the highway.

We had to cut one woman out of her car. We acted fast, but she was

seriously hurt. The ambulance took her to hospital. I hope she will

recover.

4 **Mar. 18**

Today was a nice day. I visited a school to give the students a talk

about fire safety. They all **paid attention**, and I think they learned a

lot. Now if they are ever in a fire, they will know what to do.

_____3. **What is another word for "seriously" in the reading?**
   (A) Slowly.   (B) Sadly.   (C) Badly.   (D) Truly.

_____4. **Which of these is the opposite of "recover"?**
   (A) Get better.   (B) Get bigger.
   (C) Get smaller.   (D) Get worse.

_____5. **Which of these is another way to say "paid attention"?**
   (A) Made a mess.   (B) Answered correctly.
   (C) Listened carefully.   (D) Went to sleep.

« Agree or disagree?

Agreeing to Disagree

1 Good afternoon.

2 My speech today is about pet peeves. We don't always agree on everything. Maybe you hate my favorite movie. Maybe I think your shoes don't go with your **outfit**. But if there is one thing we can often agree on, it's pet peeves.

3 For example, who enjoys watching someone eat with their mouth open? No one wants to see your food. But this happens all the time!

4 Another **common** pet peeve is interruptions. We all know the type of person. They just can't let you finish your story. And the worst thing is: they never have anything **valuable** to add. Usually it is something like "I saw that movie, too!" Great, but what is the **rush** to tell me?

⌄ interruption

« eating with one's mouth open

5 Finally, there are the people who are always late. You want to see the new **blockbuster**. You buy the tickets. But one friend is never on-time. And that's not all because you also need to stand outside and wait to give them their ticket.

6 You may have different pet peeves than I do. But we all have them. And this can help bring us together.

7 Thank you.

QUESTIONS

_____1. **What does "blockbuster" mean in the fifth paragraph?**
(A) A school program.   (B) A popular movie.
(C) A shopping center.   (D) A library.

_____2. **What is a word with the opposite meaning of "valuable" in the fourth paragraph?**
(A) Sad.   (B) New.   (C) Surprising.   (D) Useless.

_____3. **What is a word with the same meaning as "common" in the fourth paragraph?**
(A) Popular.   (B) Confusing. (C) Old.   (D) Clear.

_____4. **What does "outfit" mean in the second paragraph?**
(A) Face.   (B) Clothes.   (C) Computer.   (D) Car.

_____5. **What is a word with the same meaning as "rush" in the fourth paragraph?**
(A) Anger.   (B) Speed.   (C) Hurry.   (D) Thought.

UNIT
3

Study Strategies

3-1

Visual Material

3-2

Reference Sources

Visual material like charts and graphs, and reference sources like indexes and dictionaries, all provide important information. What's more, they help you understand complicated information more quickly than you can by reading. In this unit, you will learn to use them to gather information.

» a food blogger managing their website

Eat, Write, Post!

1 Do you love food? Do you love taking pictures of food? Do you have a talent for writing? Then perhaps you should become a food blogger! Food bloggers visit many different restaurants. Then they write about the experience on their personal blogs. They might also review street food, special snacks, and food festivals.

2 Being a food blogger is a lot of fun! But it is also hard work. Most food bloggers work alone. So they need to handle everything themselves. They take all the photos, write all the words, and manage their own websites. They also need to plan their time carefully. But with hard work comes great reward. A successful food blogger can get millions of hits on their blog and become very important in the food world!

3 See the calendar on the next page for an example of a food blogger's busy schedule. A calendar shows days and dates. For each day/date, you can add your "things-to-do" along with the time you plan to do them.

⌄ food festival

⌄ street food

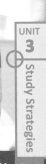

Janet's Food Blogging Calendar

2022 May, Week 1

Sunday	Monday	Tuesday	Wednesday	Thursday	Friday	Saturday
1 12 p.m. Little House Restaurant 7 p.m. Ben's Pizza Place	**2** 8 a.m. Sunny Breakfast Café 2 p.m. Mr. Wang's Beef Noodles	**3** Writing day	**4** 1 p.m. Big Juicy Burgers 9 p.m. Old Street Night Market	**5** 11 a.m. Pretty Pink Dessert Shop 5 p.m. Curry King Indian Restaurant	**6** Writing day	**7** 1 p.m.–6 p.m. Japanese Food Fair at Green Park

Q UESTIONS

_____1. **Where will Janet eat at 8 a.m. on Monday, May 2?**
(A) Little House Restaurant.   (B) Curry King Indian Restaurant.
(C) Mr. Wang's Beef Noodles.   (D) Sunny Breakfast Café.

_____2. **What time will Janet visit the Pretty Pink Dessert Shop on Thursday?**
(A) One o'clock in the afternoon.   (B) Eleven o'clock in the morning.
(C) Seven o'clock in the evening.   (D) Eight o'clock in the morning.

_____3. **Which days will Janet keep free for writing her blog?**
(A) Tuesday and Friday.   (B) Saturday and Sunday.
(C) Monday and Wednesday.   (D) Tuesday and Thursday.

_____4. **What time will Janet be working until on Saturday?**
(A) One o'clock in the afternoon.   (B) Nine o'clock at night.
(C) Six o'clock in the evening.   (D) Five o'clock in the evening.

_____5. **Which of the following is most likely TRUE about Wednesday, May 4?**
(A) Janet will eat pizza for lunch.
(B) Janet will need to get up early in the morning.
(C) Janet won't take any pictures for her blog that day.
(D) Janet won't be home until late at night.

32

» Edinburgh of the
Seven Seas

A Village Far, Far Away

1   Edinburgh of the Seven Seas is the only village on the tiny island of Tristan da Cunha. The island lies far, far out in the middle of the Atlantic Ocean. It has no airport. To get there you must take a boat from South Africa. The journey takes six days. The nearest people live 2,173 km away on another island called St. Helena. This makes Edinburgh of the Seven Seas the most remote village on Earth.

2   But for 250 people, Edinburgh of the Seven Seas is home. Look at the map on the next page. A map is a simple picture of a place. On this map, there are numbers. The box on the right tells you what buildings these numbers represent. You can see there is a school, a hospital, and two churches. To make a living, people on the island farm, fish, or work in the crawfish factory by the beach.

3   Yes, it is far away from the rest of the world. But life in this remote village isn't so different after all.

⌄ Edinburgh of the Seven Seas is the most remote village on Earth.

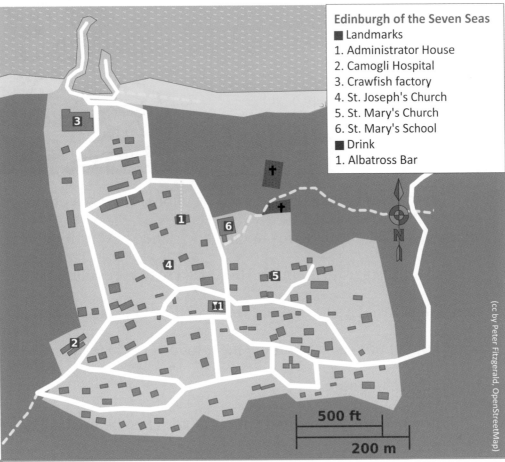

Edinburgh of the Seven Seas
■ Landmarks
1. Administrator House
2. Camogli Hospital
3. Crawfish factory
4. St. Joseph's Church
5. St. Mary's Church
6. St. Mary's School
■ Drink
1. Albatross Bar

500 ft
200 m

(cc by Peter Fitzgerald, OpenStreetMap)

Q UESTIONS

_____1. **About how long is the village from west to east?**

(A) 600 m.   (B) 200 m.   (C) 2 km.   (D) 60 m.

_____2. **What does the yellow section on the top of the map most likely represent?**

(A) A mountain.   (B) A river.

(C) A beach.   (D) A field.

_____3. **What does the number 2 show on the map?**

(A) The village school.   (B) The village hospital.

(C) One of the village churches. (D) The village bar.

_____4. **Which of the following is TRUE?**

(A) St Mary's Church is on the western side of the village.

(B) Administrator House is north of the crawfish factory.

(C) Camogli Hospital is next to St Mary's School.

(D) The Albatross Bar is south of St. Mary's School.

_____5. **Which of these buildings is closest to St Mary's School?**

(A) The crawfish factory.   (B) Administrator House.

(C) The Albatross Bar.   (D) Camogli Hospital.

UNIT **3** 🎧 (33)

33

» Instagram photos

Follow Me!

1   Henry loves to take photos with his phone. He takes photos of himself, his cat, his food, his family, his friends—everything! He recently opened an Instagram account. He started with zero followers, but at the end of just five days he had 104 followers! Henry was interested to see what kind of photos got him the most followers. So for the next five days he took careful notes.

2   In the morning, he posted a new photo. Then before bed, he recorded how many total followers he had. On day one, he posted a picture of himself in sunglasses. On day two, a photo of his lunch—some delicious soup dumplings. On day three, a photo of him and his friends at the beach. On day four, a picture of his cat, Mimi, with her toy mouse. And on day five, a picture of his grandmother in the kitchen.

3   Look at this line graph of his results and answer the questions below. A line graph shows numbers as points. A line then joins these points together so you can see how the numbers change over time.

« Instagram followers

⌃ dumpling soup

Henry's Total Instagram Followers

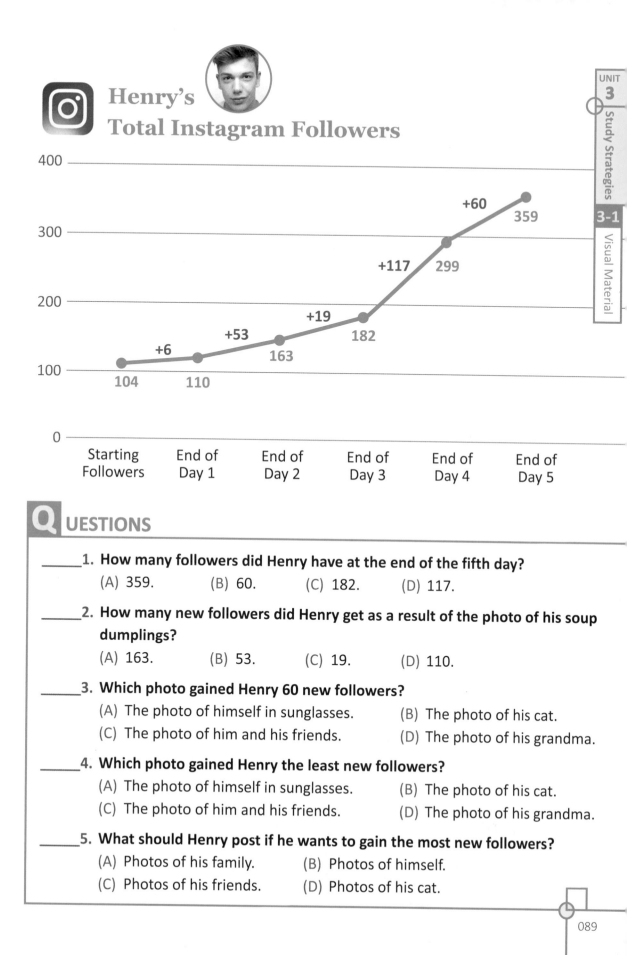

QUESTIONS

_____ 1. How many followers did Henry have at the end of the fifth day?

    (A) 359.   (B) 60.   (C) 182.   (D) 117.

_____ 2. How many new followers did Henry get as a result of the photo of his soup dumplings?

    (A) 163.   (B) 53.   (C) 19.   (D) 110.

_____ 3. Which photo gained Henry 60 new followers?

    (A) The photo of himself in sunglasses.   (B) The photo of his cat.

    (C) The photo of him and his friends.   (D) The photo of his grandma.

_____ 4. Which photo gained Henry the least new followers?

    (A) The photo of himself in sunglasses.   (B) The photo of his cat.

    (C) The photo of him and his friends.   (D) The photo of his grandma.

_____ 5. What should Henry post if he wants to gain the most new followers?

    (A) Photos of his family.   (B) Photos of himself.

    (C) Photos of his friends.   (D) Photos of his cat.

34 Selling Snacks at the Weekend

1   Annie recently started her own food truck business. So far the business is doing well. But Annie has a problem. Her food truck is quite small. Sometimes she sells out of certain items early. She wants to know what items will be popular on which day. That way she can bring more of them along with her and not sell out so early.

2   To help figure this out, last weekend, Annie recorded her sales for each day in a bar graph (below). A bar graph shows numbers as bars of different sizes and colors. This makes it easy to compare different numbers.

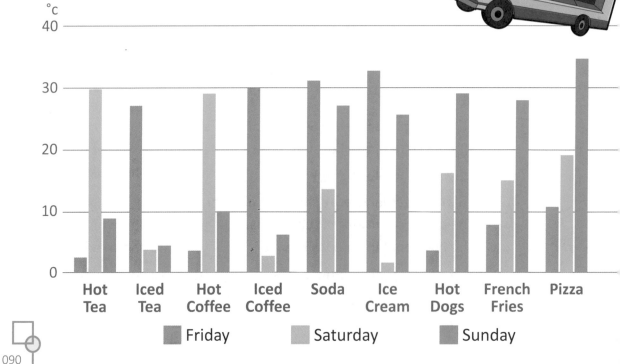

Annie's Food Truck Sales, Fri–Sun

■ Friday   ■ Saturday   ■ Sunday

≪ snack

≫ food truck

3   Annie also took notes on the weather. On Friday, the weather was hot and sunny (temperature: 32°C). On Saturday, it rained heavily and was cold (temperature: 13°C). Sunday was a beautiful day. It was sunny and cool (temperature: 18°C).

4   With this information, Annie can now better prepare for the coming week.

Q UESTIONS

_____**1. How many cups of hot coffee did Annie sell on Sunday?**
    (A) 25.   (B) 10.   (C) 5.   (D) 15.

_____**2. What was Annie's best-selling item on Friday?**
    (A) Ice cream.   (B) Hot coffee.   (C) French fries.   (D) Iced tea.

_____**3. What was the most popular drink item on Saturday?**
    (A) Hot tea.   (B) Iced coffee.   (C) Hot coffee.   (D) Soda.

_____**4. Which of the following does the graph show us?**
    (A) Food items sell well on very nice days.
    (B) People like to buy hot drinks on hot days.
    (C) Lots of people buy ice cream on cold days.
    (D) People buy more soda when the temperature is lower.

_____**5. Tomorrow, the weather will be very hot. Which of the following items should Annie prepare less of?**
    (A) Ice cream.   (B) Soda.   (C) Hot dogs.   (D) Iced tea.

35

Where's All the Water?

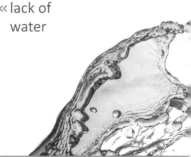

« lack of water

1   Taiwan is running out of water! Taiwan gets most of its water from typhoons. But in 2020, no typhoons hit the island. And as climate change makes the world drier, Taiwan can expect fewer and fewer typhoons in the future. Taiwan also has some of the lowest water prices in the world. Therefore, people often waste water and think nothing of it. We must change our bad habits now!

2   So, what can each of us do to save water? Take a look at the pie chart on the next page. A pie chart shows numbers as pieces of a circle. The bigger the piece of pie, the bigger the number. Can you believe we use most of our household water on flushing the toilet? One great way to use less water is to collect the water from your shower in a bucket. You can then use that shower water to flush your toilet. That way you are cutting down your water usage by more than a quarter! If we all save water together, we can keep Taiwan's future drought free!

» typhoon

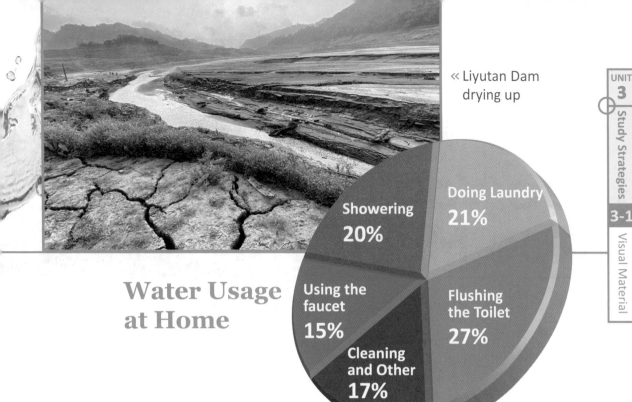

Water Usage at Home

Showering
20%

Doing Laundry
21%

Using the faucet
15%

Flushing the Toilet
27%

Cleaning and Other
17%

Q UESTIONS

_____1. **In the pie chart, what does the green slice show?**
   (A) How much water we use cleaning.
   (B) How much water we use flushing the toilet.
   (C) How much water we use doing laundry.
   (D) How much water we use showering.

_____2. **Doing laundry uses how much of a house's water?**
   (A) 27 percent.   (B) 21 percent.
   (C) 20 percent.   (D) 15 percent.

_____3. **What activity uses 20 percent of a house's water?**
   (A) Showering.   (B) Flushing the toilet.
   (C) Using the faucet.   (D) Cleaning and Other.

_____4. **Which of the following uses the least amount of water?**
   (A) Showering.   (B) Flushing the toilet.
   (C) Using the faucet.   (D) Cleaning and other.

_____5. **Which of the following is TRUE?**
   (A) Cleaning uses more than 20 percent of a house's water.
   (B) The chart's blue slice shows how much water we use doing laundry.
   (C) Showering and laundry use less water than flushing the toilet.
   (D) Flushing the toilet and showering use almost half a house's water.

36

» a messy room

Do You Have Too Much Stuff?

1 Is your bedroom a mess? Maybe it is time you decluttered your life! Decluttering means throwing away the things you don't need. Having fewer possessions is good for your mind and mood. But decluttering isn't always easy. Luckily, there are many books that will teach you how to declutter your room. On the next page is the table of contents from one such book, *Less is Best* by Lisa McClean. A table of contents shows you the name of each chapter in a book. It also gives you the page number for each chapter. With a little help from Lisa, you too can declutter your own personal environment.

QUESTIONS

_____1. On which page does "Chapter 3 Books" begin?

(A) 25.   (B) 37.   (C) 6.   (D) 80.

_____2. In which chapter would you learn how to throw away clothes?

(A) Chapter 4.   (B) Chapter 2.
(C) Chapter 6.   (D) Chapter 7.

_____3. You know how to choose what to keep and what to throw away. So you decide you will declutter your house over the weekend. Which chapters should you read to prepare for this?

(A) Chapters 1 and 2.   (B) Chapters 9 and 10.
(C) Chapters 6 and 7.   (D) Chapters 4 and 5.

⌃ a tidy display   ⌃ decluttering

Contents

_____4. **You threw away a lot of your old stuff. Now you feel sad.
Which page should you turn to?**

(A) 3.   (B) 56.   (C) 102.   (D) 132.

_____5. **Which of these is TRUE about Chapter 1?**

(A) It begins on page 3.

(B) It is ten pages long.

(C) It is the first part of the book.

(D) It is about choosing what to throw away.

37 A Brief History of the Console Wars

≫ Magnavox Odyssey
(cc by Evan-Amos)

≫ playing video games

1 The first home videogame console came out in 1972. Its name was the Magnavox Odyssey, and it cost the same as about $600 dollars. What did you get for your money? Only 28 games, and most of them were very simple. No wonder only 350,000 people bought one.

2 Back then, video games were totally new. You didn't play them because they were super fun. You played them because they were strange (that is, if you could play them at all). Not many people owned a video game console in those early years.

3 Now, everyone from your best friend to your grandmother plays video games. Whether on a smartphone or a video game console, we all love to play. It used to be strange to play video games. Now it is strange not to play them. Just think: the PlayStation 4 sold over 115 million consoles in its lifetime. That is a whole lot more than the Magnavox Odyssey!

4 Take a look at the timeline below. A timeline lists events in order from earliest to latest. This one lists some popular video game consoles and the dates they came out.

» PlayStation 5

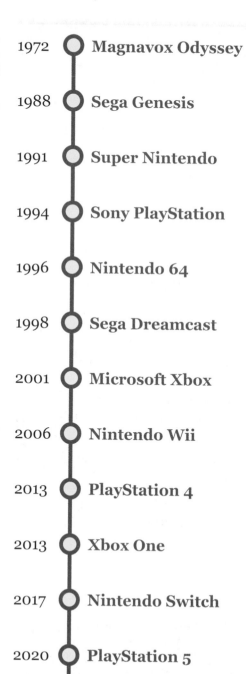

1972	**Magnavox Odyssey**
1988	**Sega Genesis**
1991	**Super Nintendo**
1994	**Sony PlayStation**
1996	**Nintendo 64**
1998	**Sega Dreamcast**
2001	**Microsoft Xbox**
2006	**Nintendo Wii**
2013	**PlayStation 4**
2013	**Xbox One**
2017	**Nintendo Switch**
2020	**PlayStation 5**

QUESTIONS

_____1. **Based on the timeline, which is the oldest console?**
(A) PlayStation.
(B) Sega Genesis.
(C) Nintendo Wii.
(D) Microsoft Xbox

_____2. **Based on the timeline, when was Xbox One released?**
(A) 2017.　　(B) 2001.
(C) 2020.　　(D) 2013.

_____3. **Based on the timeline, when was Nintendo Wii released?**
(A) 2013.　　(B) 1991.
(C) 2006.　　(D) 2017.

_____4. **Based on the timeline, which is the newest console?**
(A) Super Nintendo.
(B) Sega Dreamcast.
(C) Sega Genesis.
(D) Nintendo Wii.

_____5. **Based on the timeline, what console was released the same year as Xbox One?**
(A) Nintendo Switch.
(B) PlayStation 4.
(C) Sega Dreamcast.
(D) Super Nintendo.

38

» microwave

Mix! Zap! Yum!

1 Brownies are my favorite snack. They are sweet, delicious, and easy to make at home! Usually to make brownies you need an oven. However, in Taiwan, it isn't common to have an oven in your kitchen. So how do I make my own brownies? I use a microwave!

2 Using just a few easy ingredients, a microwave, and a cup, you too can make delicious brownies at home. Take a look at the recipe on the next page! A recipe gives you a list of ingredients and tells you step-by-step how to make a dish.

QUESTIONS

_____ 1. **How long does this recipe take to make?**
(A) Less than 60 seconds.   (B) More than five minutes.
(C) Less than five minutes.   (D) A little over 60 seconds.

_____ 2. **How much sugar do you need to make this recipe?**
(A) Fifty grams.   (B) Thirty grams.
(C) Two tablespoons.   (D) Just a pinch.

_____ 3. **Step 2 says "Add the wet ingredients and mix well." How many wet ingredients are there in this recipe?**
(A) Four.   (B) Five.   (C) Three.   (D) Two.

Microwave Brownie in a Cup

⌄ brownie

Total time: Less than 5 mins
Serves: 1

Ingredients

Dry
- flour (30 g)
- sugar (50 g)
- cocoa powder (2 tablespoons)
- salt (a pinch)
- cinnamon (a pinch)

Wet
- water (60 ml)
- melted butter (30 ml)

Toppings
- ice cream / sprinkles / marshmallows / strawberries

⌄ cocoa powder

⌄ cinnamon

⌄ marshmallows

Method

Step 1: Add the dry ingredients to a cup and mix well.

Step 2: **Add the wet ingredients and mix well.**

Step 3: Cook in the microwave for 60 seconds. (You might need to cook it for a little longer if your microwave is not very powerful.)

Step 4: Let it cool and then add your toppings.

Step 5: Eat!

_____ 4. **What should you do next after you cook the ingredients in the microwave?**
  (A) Eat the brownie.　　(B) Add the dry ingredients.
  (C) Let the brownie cool down.　(D) Wash the brownie.

_____ 5. **Which of these do you NOT need to make this recipe?**
  (A) Butter.　(B) A cup.　(C) Flour.　(D) An oven.

39

» a thesaurus entry

Many Words, One Meaning

1 The English language has a lot of words. It is impossible to know exactly how many, but we think at least a quarter of a million! Of course, you don't have to learn them all! Around 9,000 words cover 98 percent of everyday English. But that is still a lot! When you are trying to learn all these words, it can help to group words with similar meanings together.

2 Take the word *hard*, for example. What are some other words for *hard*? Well, there is *difficult, challenging, tough*. Are there any more? Let's look in a thesaurus to find out! A thesaurus is a book full of synonyms (words with the same meaning). What's more, a thesaurus gives you a list of antonyms (words with the opposite meaning) as well. Each entry lists these synonyms and antonyms in alphabetical order (from A to Z).

⌄ There are lots of words in the English language.

imerical, empty,
ginary, unauthor-
ded, unjustified,
unwarranted

s, cornerstone,
entals, prelimi-
work, underpin-

assemblage,
nch, category,
luster, collec-
on, coterie,
g, gathering,
troop ~v. 2.
ssort, brack-
er, marshal,
ange, sort 3.
er, congre-
ather, get

(SI.), food,
victuals

grubby bes
grimy, manky
mucky, scruf.
smutty, soiled
untidy, unwash

grudge 1. n. al
aversion, bitterr
ance, hard feelir
lence, malice, pic
spite, venom 2. v
complain, covet,
resent, stint

gruelling arduou:
crushing, demandin
fatiguing, fierce, g
laborious, punishing
ous, taxing

hard

1. *a.* difficult to do or understand

   Synonyms: baffling, challenging, complex, complicated, difficult, impenetrable, intricate, involved, problematic, puzzling, tough, tangled

   Antonyms: clear, easy, simple

2. *a.* not soft

   Synonyms: compact, dense, firm, inflexible, rigid, solid, strong, tough, unyielding

   Antonyms: flexible, malleable, pliable, soft

QUESTIONS

_____1. How many other words for *hard* (meaning *not soft*) does this thesaurus give?

(A) Twelve. (B) Nine. (C) Three. (D) Thirteen.

_____2. Which of these is another word for *hard* (meaning *difficult to do or understand*)?

(A) Complex. (B) Simple. (C) Firm. (D) Flexible.

_____3. What is TRUE about the word *solid*?

(A) It is a synonym of *hard* (meaning *difficult to do or understand*).

(B) It is an antonym of *hard* (meaning *not soft*).

(C) It is an antonym of *hard* (meaning *difficult to do or understand*).

(D) It is a synonym of *hard* (meaning *not soft*).

_____4. Which word is a synonym for both *hard* (meaning *difficult to do or understand*) and *hard* (meaning *not soft*)?

(A) Strong. (B) Tangled. (C) Tough. (D) Compact.

_____5. Another word for *hard* (meaning *difficult to do or understand*) is *perplexing*. Where would *perplexing* appear in this thesaurus entry?

(A) Between *malleable* and *pliable*.

(B) Between *involved* and *problematic*.

(C) Between *easy* and *simple*.

(D) Between *baffling* and *challenging*.

» Demon Slayer manga

40 Monster Killer!

1 Do you know about *Demon Slayer: Kimetsu no Yaiba*? It is a very popular manga and anime series from Japan. The story is about a young boy, Tanjiro Kamado. One day, a demon kills his family and turns his younger sister into a demon. Tanjiro promises to kill the demon and turn his sister back into a human.

2 The manga is one of the best-selling manga series of all time. And the first season of the anime series won many awards. A very popular *Demon Slayer* movie also came out in 2020. Are you interested in learning more? To find out more about *Demon Slayer*, search for "Demon Slayer: Kimetsu no Yaiba" in an online search engine. When you perform the search, you will get a list of search results like the one below. Each result shows the website address and some information about what is on the website.

⌃ poster of *Demon Slayer: Mugen Train*

⌃ *Demon Slayer* T-shirt

www.toottoot.com/demon-slayer-season-1

Watch Season 1 of Demon Slayer Online

Sign up to TootToot to watch episodes of Demon Slayer and other popular TV shows now. The first month is free . . .

www.animestore.com/demon-slayer-kimetsu-no-yaiba

Demon Slayer Toys and Clothes for Sale

Demon Slayer T-shirts and hats, plus action figures of all your favorite Demon Slayer characters—Tanjiro . . .

www.demonslayerfans.com

Everything You Want to Know about Demon Slayer

HISTORY | STORY | CHARACTERS | MANGA | ANIME | MOVIE --- This is a site by Demon Slayer fans, for Demon Slayer fans. Here you'll find information about everything, from the manga's writer to . . .

www.fivestars.com/demon-slayer-mugen-train

Demon Slayer – Movie Review by Dan Sharpe –

★ ★ ★ ★ ★

I am a big fan of the Demon Slayer anime. So when I heard about the movie, I was so excited. And guess what? I loved it! The movie begins . . .

www.tvnews.com/demon-slayer-season-2

Demon Slayer Season 2 Coming Soon – What We Know So Far

Season 2 of the popular Demon Slayer anime series is almost here! The new season will start in just two weeks. Here at TV News we have some special information about what will happen in the future story . . .

Q UESTIONS

_____1. **You want to watch an episode of *Demon Slayer*. Which website should you visit?**

    (A) www.animestore.com   (B) www.demonslayerfans.com

    (C) www.fivestars.com   (D) www.toottoot.com

_____2. **What would you find on the site www.animestore.com?**

    (A) Clothes with *Demon Slayer* pictures on them.

    (B) Someone's opinion about the *Demon Slayer* movie.

    (C) News about the new season of *Demon Slayer*.

    (D) Information about the characters in *Demon Slayer*.

_____3. **You want to find out who wrote the *Demon Slayer* manga. Which website should you visit?**

    (A) www.animestore.com   (B) www.demonslayerfans.com

    (C) www.tvnews.com   (D) www.toottoot.com

_____4. **Which of the following can we learn from the website www.tvnews.com?**

    (A) How long the *Demon Slayer* movie was.

    (B) How much a *Demon Slayer* T-shirt costs.

    (C) Who wrote the *Demon Slayer* manga.

    (D) When the new season of *Demon Slayer* will begin.

_____5. **What do we know about Dan Sharpe?**

    (A) He bought a *Demon Slayer* hat last week.

    (B) He is one of the voice actors in *Demon Slayer*.

    (C) He enjoyed the *Demon Slayer* movie.

    (D) He knows what will happen in season 2 of *Demon Slayer*.

UNIT
4

Final Review

41 ⌄ Catherine II (1762-1796)

A Truly Great Woman

1 Catherine II was one of Russia's greatest leaders. She came to power in 1762 and ruled Russia for 34 years until her death in 1796.

2 Catherine did many important things during her time in power. Even though she was not born in Russia, she loved the country very much. And she wanted to see it become strong, rich, and cultured.

3 Catherine believed in the power of education. She thought Russia would become great if its people improved their minds.

Q UESTIONS

_____ 1. **What is the writer's main point?**
   (A) Catherine II wanted to see Russia become a richer country.
   (B) By the time Catherine II died, Russia controlled much more land than before
   (C) Catherine II was a great leader and did many important things for Russia.
   (D) Catherine II supported many artists and scientists during her time in power

_____ 2. **Which of the following is TRUE about the schools Catherine set up in 1786?**
   (A) Students had to pay a lot of money to study there.
   (B) Both boys and girls could study there.
   (C) Only poor children could study there.
   (D) The schools were all in one city.

_____ 3. **How does the writer end the passage?**
   (A) With an interesting fact.   (B) With a funny story.
   (C) With a difficult question.   (D) With a wish for the future.

» The Russian Empire in 1792. Catherine increased Russia's land significantly through a mix of diplomacy and war.

So she set about modernizing education across Russia. In 1786, she established hundreds of free schools across the country. These schools were open to boys and girls, whether rich or poor. She also supported many artists and scientists. So during her time in power, art and science in Russia thrived.

4   Furthermore, through a clever mix of diplomacy and war, Catherine greatly increased Russia's lands. By the time she died, Russia controlled large areas of Southeastern Europe and even parts of North America.

5   Under Catherine, Russia became one of the strongest and most important countries in Europe. As a result, the Russian people now call her Catherine the Great!

_____ **4. What is probably TRUE about Catherine II?**
- (A) She did not like being the leader of Russia.
- (B) She never went to school herself.
- (C) She was a popular leader.
- (D) She died poor.

_____ **5. What was the effect of Catherine's time in power?**
- (A) Russia became a weak country with few friends in Europe.
- (B) Russia's business people became richer, but the common people remained poor.
- (C) Fewer people went to school than before, and art and science almost disappeared.
- (D) Russia became one of the strongest and most important countries in Europe.

42 Wear it Well!

https://www.stayhappyandhealthy.com

Home > COVID-19 > Masks >

» wearing a mask

1   Wearing a mask is very important while COVID-19 is still not under control. When you wear a mask, you protect yourself from catching the disease. But more importantly, if you have the disease, a mask stops you giving it to other people. To make sure your mask works, you must wear it correctly. Many people don't know how to wear a mask correctly. This makes the masks useless.

7 Steps to Wearing Your Mask Correctly

1. Clean your hands well before you touch your mask.
2. Make sure the white side is on the inside and the side with a color is on the outside.

3. Pull the loops over your ears.
4. Place your mask over your nose and mouth and pull it down over your chin.

5. Push down on the metal wire so it fits the shape of your nose.
6. Make sure the mask is not too loose. If it is, make the loops smaller.
7. Make sure you can breathe easily. If you find it hard to breathe, you might need to get a larger mask.

Q UESTIONS

_____1. **What is the main point of the reading?**

(A) If you don't wear a mask properly, the mask becomes useless.

(B) Please wear a mask correctly to stop the spread of COVID-19.

(C) Many people don't know how to wear a mask correctly.

(D) The white side of the mask should be on the inside.

_____2. **What is the writer's purpose in writing this passage?**

(A) To teach the reader how to do something.

(B) To make the reader laugh.

(C) To explain the meaning of a word.

(D) To invite the reader to do something fun.

_____3. **Which of these should you do before you put on a mask?**

(A) Wash your face.   (B) Clean your hands.

(C) Take some medicine.   (D) Blow your nose.

_____4. **How does the writer order the 7 steps in the reading?**

(A) From first to last.   (B) From easiest to most difficult.

(C) From A to Z.   (D) From least important to most important.

_____5. **Which of these pictures could appear next to Step 4?**

(A)    (B)

(C)    (D)

« spicy food

43

Too Spicy?
Not Anymore!

1   Like a lot of people, I love spicy food! The problem is that the burning can get too much for me sometimes! My mouth feels like it is on fire! I just want to drink cup after cup of ice water, but it does not seem to work. I have to sit in pain until the burning goes away while everyone else is enjoying their food!

2   But scientists now know the answer to my painful problem—milk! Chili peppers are full of the chemical capsaicin. That's what causes that burning feeling in my mouth. Capsaicin doesn't dissolve in water. So no matter how much water I drink, the capsaicin stays on my tongue. But it *does* dissolve in milk. So if I take a mouthful of milk, it will wash the capsaicin away and the burning in my mouth will stop. Other than milk, drinks with lots of sugar also have a similar effect.

⌄ dissolve

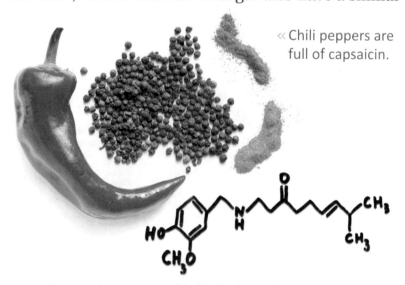

« Chili peppers are full of capsaicin.

3 Now that I know the solution, I'll never have to suffer through a spicy meal ever again! I can finally eat as much spicy food as I want!

» Milk can wash away capsaicin.

QUESTIONS

_____ **1. How does the writer begin the passage?**
(A) By telling you about his own experience.
(B) By telling you an interesting fact.
(C) By telling you a surprising number.
(D) By telling you a sad story.

_____ **2. What is the writer trying to do in this article?**
(A) Teach you about an interesting time in history.
(B) Make you feel hope for the future.
(C) Show you a serious problem in the world.
(D) Tell you about a new answer to a problem.

_____ **3. Which of the following is TRUE?**
(A) Drinking milk won't stop the burning feeling in your mouth.
(B) Drinking water won't stop the burning feeling in your mouth.
(C) No one knows how to stop the burning feeling from eating spicy food.
(D) Putting salt on your tongue can stop the burning feeling in your mouth.

_____ **4. Based on the second paragraph, which of these would most likely get rid of the burning feeling in your mouth?**
(A) Hot green tea.　　(B) Black coffee.
(C) Orange juice.　　(D) Sweet milk tea.

_____ **5. How will the information in the article change the writer's life?**
(A) He can never eat spicy food again.
(B) He can never drink milk again.
(C) He can now eat as much spicy food as he wants.
(D) He can eat in restaurants every day of the week.

» succulents

^ watering a succulent

Plant Care 101 for Succulents

1   Do you know about succulents? They are a beautiful type of plant, and they can really brighten up a room. You should get one! But if you do, make sure to take good care of it. Here are some tips:

1 Put the succulent in a sunny spot. It needs about six hours of sunlight each day.

2 Turn the plant often. This makes sure all sides of the succulent get enough sun.

3 Water the dirt, not the leaves.

4 Keep the plant clean. Too much dust on the leaves makes it hard for the plant to grow.

5 Make sure water doesn't sit at the bottom of the pot.

6 Use the right dirt. Make sure it doesn't hold too much water.

7 Don't let bugs eat your succulent! Keeping the dirt dry helps keep the bugs away.

8 Use different amounts of water for different seasons. Succulents grow during the spring and rest during the fall and winter. When it comes to water, just remember: "**spring forward, fall back**."

⌃ a bug eating a succulent

Q UESTIONS

_____1. **According to the article, what happens if there's too much dust on a succulent's leaves?**
   (A) The plant turns green.   (B) The plant has trouble growing.
   (C) The plant needs less water.   (D) The plant holds too much water.

_____2. **What could this article best be described as?**
   (A) A news story.   (B) A list.
   (C) A personal story.   (D) A report.

_____3. **What is the writer's tone in the first paragraph?**
   (A) Loving.   (B) Excited.   (C) Angry.   (D) Serious.

_____4. **What does "spring forward, fall back" likely mean in the final paragraph?**
   (A) Most succulents only last one year, and die during fall.
   (B) Spring is a popular time for people to buy succulents.
   (C) Water the succulent more during spring, and less during fall.
   (D) Water the succulent's leaves during spring, and its dirt during fall.

_____5. **What is the main idea of the article?**
   (A) Succulents are a very difficult plant to take care of.
   (B) Follow these eight easy tips to keep your succulents healthy.
   (C) Succulents are a type of plant unlike any other.
   (D) How to make a room more beautiful using plants.

45
More Than Smiles and Colorful Uniforms

» female cheerleaders doing stunts

1   Can you think of some **high-risk** sports? You're probably thinking about things like American football or ice hockey, right? Not cheerleading. That's just pretty girls dancing around, isn't it? Think again!

2   Cheerleading is a very serious activity indeed. Female cheerleaders must complete difficult stunts, often many meters above the ground. Male cheerleaders have to lift female cheerleaders high in the air. They have to hold them safely and catch them before they fall. And they must all do this while looking **bright and sunny** for those watching. Therefore, cheerleaders need to be very strong.

⌄ cheerleaders

They must also have great balance and focus. **One wrong move** can result in a cheerleader getting very hurt.

3   As a result, cheerleading is one of the most dangerous sports around. Over half of all the worst accidents in female athletes happen in cheerleading. So although it looks like a fun activity, cheerleading certainly isn't for the **faint of heart**. It is not just smiles and colorful uniforms. It is a difficult sport with **real** dangers!

Q UESTIONS

_____1. **Which is another word for "high-risk"?**
  (A) Easy.   (B) Heavy.   (C) Friendly.   (D) Dangerous.

_____2. **What is the opposite of "bright and sunny"?**
  (A) Unhappy.   (B) Glad.   (C) Afraid.   (D) Hungry.

_____3. **What does the writer mean by the phrase "one wrong move" in the second paragraph?**
  (A) A difficult question.   (B) A long wait.
  (C) A quiet sound.   (D) A small mistake.

_____4. **If someone is "faint of heart," what are they?**
  (A) Happy to work in a team.   (B) Afraid to do dangerous things.
  (C) Tired from working too hard. (D) Excited to be doing something.

_____5. **What is another word for "real" in the final sentence?**
  (A) Small.   (B) Careful.   (C) Serious.   (D) Weak.

46 Jobs For Teens?

Martin Cho 1d ago

I just watched this interesting video. I agree with a lot of it. I loved having a job when I was a teenager. What do you all think?

Video: Why Teenagers Should Get a Job | [10 minutes]

Q UESTIONS

_____ 1. **What does Tina Wei mean by the word "one"?**
(A) A job.   (B) A video.   (C) A test.   (D) A young person.

_____ 2. **What does it mean if you work "part-time"?**
(A) You work for a big company.
(B) You work with your hands.
(C) You only work for some of the week.
(D) You work in an office with lots of other people.

_____ 3. **What is another word for "normal"?**
(A) Wrong.   (B) Useful.   (C) Successful. (D) Common.

_____ 4. **What does Rick mean by "it"?**
(A) Reading comics all day.   (B) Working in a restaurant.
(C) Staying home.   (D) Hating his job.

💬 **13 Comments**

Roy Wang

I'm fifteen and I really want a job. I would love to have my own money to spend on things I want. But my mom won't let me.☹

Tina Wei

Roy Wang I agree with your mother. Students in Taiwan need to study for their tests. They don't have time for one.

Gina Chen

Tina Wei Not even a part-time job? Working for a few hours on a Saturday or Sunday won't affect students' school work too much.

Jenny Jones

It's normal in the United States for teenagers to have jobs. It teaches them to be independent. I think it's a positive thing.

Rick Smith

My dad made me get a job at a restaurant when I was 15. I hated it. I just wanted to stay home and play videos games. It did teach me some good life lessons, though.

_____ 5. **Here are the first few sentences from the video "Why Teenagers Should Get a Job."**

"I'm Jason. I'm sixteen, and I work Saturday mornings in a clothing store. It's hard sometimes, but I love it. And I think I am a better person because of it. The work is only a few hours a week, but I'm learning so many things I would never learn in the classroom. In this video I want to share with you all the valuable life skills I have learned."

What is the opposite of "valuable"?

(A) Useless.   (B) Strong.   (C) Proud.   (D) Mean.

Getting to Know You

Rachel is in her final year of high school. She recently sent out some college applications. One of the colleges asked her to do a short interview. Below are some of the questions the interviewer asked her, along with her responses.

⌄ school subjects

Interviewer: Why are you interested in this college?

Rachel: Math is my favorite subject. And recently I read a book called *The Magic of Numbers* by Professor Grace Jones. She teaches at this college. I thought her ideas were so **fascinating**. I would love to study under her.

Interviewer: What subject in high school do you find most difficult?

Rachel: History. Remembering all the different dates is really hard. But I **devised** a study method to help me. I write a short funny song about each event. Then I can remember the dates easily.

GEOGRAPHY

LITERATURE

DRAWING

BIOLOGY

Interviewer: What will you do to make our college a better place?

20 **Rachel:** I love live music, so I would love to help organize music shows. I think **they** would be good environments for students to make new friends.

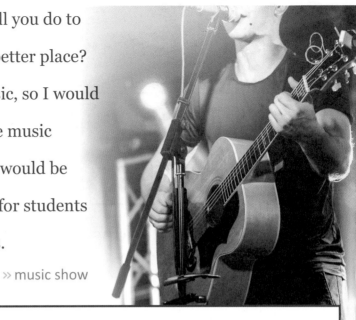

» music show

QUESTIONS

_____1. **What is another word for "responses"?**
(A) Questions.   (B) Subjects.   (C) Skills.   (D) Answers.

_____2. **What is the opposite of "fascinating"?**
(A) Boring.   (B) Interesting.   (C) Old.   (D) Young.

_____3. **Which of these means the same as "devised"?**
(A) Took away.   (B) Made up.   (C) Gave up.   (D) Fell over.

_____4. **What does the word "they" mean in the final sentence?**
(A) Important dates.   (B) Colleges.
(C) Math teachers.   (D) Live music shows.

_____5. **Here are some notes the interviewer made about Rachel.**

> **Student name:** Rachel Xu
> **Notes:**
> Wants to study math under Professor Grace Jones.
> Finds ways to succeed in difficult subjects.
> Enthusiastic about music.
> Wants to join in college life.

What does it mean if someone is "enthusiastic" about something?
(A) They have a hard time understanding something.
(B) They have a strong interest in something.
(C) They are tired of doing something.
(D) They are not happy to do something.

100 Delicious Dishes in One Book

Rich Logan's Delicious Dishes

by **Rich Logan**

★ ★ ★ ★ ⯪

Over 100 delicious recipes from the winner of the TV show "SuperChef."

Buy Now $15.99

Reviews

"Every serious home cook should own this book!"
—*Home Cook Magazine*

"Rich Logan knows how to make simple ingredients taste delicious!"
—*Food World*

"This book contains dishes from all over the world—France, China, India, Italy, the UK, and many more. If you want to learn to cook a wide range of dishes, this book is for you!"
—*Daily News Book Reviews*

"Each recipe in this book uses a simple list of ingredients and is easy to follow. So it is perfect for beginners. But experienced cooks will also learn some cool new tricks as well."
—*Good Food Monthly*

"These dishes will be familiar to experienced cooks, but Logan puts his own special twist on each one. Even though I am a long-time cook, I was still excited to try out each recipe."
—**Darius Brown, Head Chef at the *Prince Restaurant*, London**

⌃ ingredients

⌄ home cook

QUESTIONS

_____1. **What does the phrase "a wide range of dishes" most likely mean?**

  (A) Food from one country.   (B) Many different types of food.

  (C) Difficult-to-make food.   (D) Good-tasting food.

_____2. **What is another word for "follow" in the reading?**

  (A) Buy.   (B) Throw away.   (C) Write.   (D) Understand.

_____3. **Which word has the opposite meaning to "familiar" in the reading?**

  (A) Lucky.   (B) Important.   (C) Healthy.   (D) New.

_____4. **What does the writer mean by "a long-time cook"?**

  (A) A cook with a big family.   (B) A cook with his or her own TV show.

  (C) A cook with a lot of money.   (D) A cook with lots of experience.

_____5. **Eric wants to buy the book, so he click on "Buy Now." It takes him to this page.**

Thank you for your order!

Please **confirm** your address and payment method. Then click "complete order."

Home address _Change_	**Payment method** _Change_
Eric Chen	VISA (ending in 3004)
No. 185, Yongchang St.,	
Yingge Town,	
New Taipei City,	
Taiwan	

Complete Order

What does the word "confirm" most likely mean?

  (A) Fix something broken.   (B) Write something again.

  (C) Check if something is correct.   (D) Give something as a gift.

» Whales come to the surface to breathe.

49 Is a Whale Just a Big Fish?

1   Whales and fish look similar, and they share the same underwater home. This used to make people think they were the same animal. But now we know the truth: they are completely different.

2   To see just how different they are, take a look at the Venn diagram on the next page. A Venn diagram has two circles. In this one, facts about whales are in the left circle. Facts about fish are in the right circle. And where the circles overlap are facts about whales *and* fish.

3   Whales give birth to live young. They also take care of their babies for years. Fish lay hundreds of thousands of eggs, and then move on. When the eggs hatch, there is no one to protect the babies. Up to 99 percent of them will die before they grow up.

4   Whales also breathe air, unlike fish. They live underwater, but they still need to come to the surface to breathe. How long can a whale hold its breath? That depends on the whale. Killer whales come to the surface every minute or so. But a sperm whale can hold its breath for 90 minutes.

5   So maybe the better question is: Are whales the same as humans?

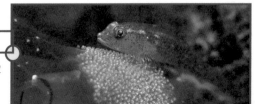

« a fish laying eggs

» killer whale

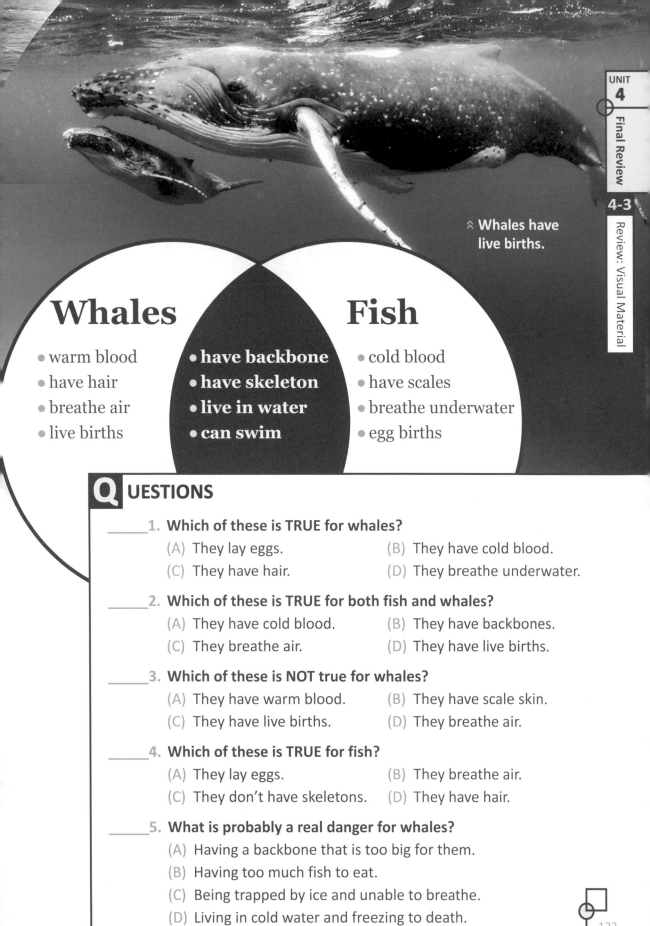

⌃ **Whales have
live births.**

Whales

- warm blood
- have hair
- breathe air
- live births

- **have backbone**
- **have skeleton**
- **live in water**
- **can swim**

Fish

- cold blood
- have scales
- breathe underwater
- egg births

Q UESTIONS

_____ 1. **Which of these is TRUE for whales?**

   (A) They lay eggs.   (B) They have cold blood.

   (C) They have hair.   (D) They breathe underwater.

_____ 2. **Which of these is TRUE for both fish and whales?**

   (A) They have cold blood.   (B) They have backbones.

   (C) They breathe air.   (D) They have live births.

_____ 3. **Which of these is NOT true for whales?**

   (A) They have warm blood.   (B) They have scale skin.

   (C) They have live births.   (D) They breathe air.

_____ 4. **Which of these is TRUE for fish?**

   (A) They lay eggs.   (B) They breathe air.

   (C) They don't have skeletons. (D) They have hair.

_____ 5. **What is probably a real danger for whales?**

   (A) Having a backbone that is too big for them.

   (B) Having too much fish to eat.

   (C) Being trapped by ice and unable to breathe.

   (D) Living in cold water and freezing to death.

A Story for Every Word

⌃ Tea was introduced to Europe in the 1600s.

1   We all know that countries have histories and buildings have histories. But did you know that words have histories, too? Some of these word-histories are quite surprising!

2   Take the English word "tea," for example. Do you know where it comes from? In the 1600s, most of the tea in Europe came from Xiamen, in China's Fujian Province, and Taiwan. When tea arrived in Europe and people asked what it was, the sellers used the Hokkien (Taiwanese) word *tê*. In Spain, this word became *té*. In France, *thé*. And in England, *tea*!

3   You can buy many books about the histories of words. Most of these books will have an index at the back (see the example on the next page). An index lists the book's important topics in alphabetical order (from A to Z). To find a topic, turn to the index, find the topic, and then turn to that page number to read about it.

» dried green tea leaves for sale at a market in Xiamen, Fujian Province

Where Do Our Words Come From?

Index

A					
alien	17	big	66	coffee	6
ant	35	bogeyman	165	crocodile	40
apple	2-4	book	91-92	curry	7
April	56	bug	35		
arrive	43	burger	3	**D**	
August	57			daisy	108
		C		dance	32
		calendar	44	December	58
B		cartoon	92	denim	208
bamboo	109	caterpillar	36-37	desire	156
beach	87	cheat	99	detail	177
beer	4			dog	39-42

QUESTIONS

_____1. On which page of the book *Where Do Our Words Come From?* would you find information about the word "August"?

(A) Page 43.　(B) Page 3.　(C) Page 58.　(D) Page 57.

_____2. What word would you find information about on page 7?

(A) Burger.　(B) Apple.　(C) Beer.　(D) Curry.

_____3. How many pages in the book are there about the word "cartoon"?

(A) One.　(B) Two.　(C) Three.　(D) Four.

_____4. Which of the following words does the book have the most information about?

(A) Crocodile.　(B) Detail.　(C) Dog.　(D) Caterpillar.

_____5. The index does not show an entry for the word "black." If it did, where would the entry be?

(A) Between "beer" and "big."

(B) Between "big" and "bogeyman."

(C) Between "bamboo" and "beach."

(D) Between "bug" and "burger."

Unit 1 ┊ 閱讀技巧

1-1 歸納要旨／找出支持性細節

01 名畫中的女子 P. 20

剛開始，我只能一窺妳的模樣
透過博物館群眾之縫隙。
妳這幅畫作比我想像的小，
用色偏暗——全是綠色調、黃色調與棕色調。
我心想，沒什麼特別的。

但當我靠近一點，可以看到妳雙眼的時候，
妳的眼神似乎如影隨形，
彷彿活生生的在我身邊，對我感興趣！
我開始心跳加速。

接下來，我站到妳面前了——
就在那兒了，妳出名的微笑！但妳是在微笑嗎？
我不太確定。我移開視線，回頭再看一次，
覺得妳似乎看起來有點悲傷，
好像是為了我們強顏歡笑。
日復一日地這麼示人。

然後我明白了。
妳的眼神——其實不是有興致。
而是感到無聊，想要趁機進入夢鄉。
因為在夢境裡，妳或許就自由了——
不受畫框、上百萬對眼睛的注視所束縛。
或許，妳就能真正發自內心微笑了。

而我只能靠想像，才能知道妳的真心微笑會有多
美。

02 麵粉的魔力 P. 22

梅為了校刊內容而訪問林先生。

梅：林先生，您是民俗藝術家，對嗎？

林先生：對，沒錯。我製作捏麵人。

梅：什麼是捏麵人呢？

林先生：它們是一種玩具，但我用糯米粉來做。

梅：太有趣了！那麼要如何製作？

林先生：我會先用雙手桿壓麵糰，也會用這種竹製工具來塑造捏麵人的身體部位。

梅：我看得出來這很講究技巧。您最受歡迎的捏麵人有哪些呢？

林先生：我做的捏麵人很多都是老故事的角色。美猴王孫悟空大概是最受歡迎的捏麵人。
但我也會做一些現代卡通人物，例如哆啦 A 夢和皮卡丘，這類捏麵人也很受歡迎。

梅：現在好像沒有很多像您這樣的藝術家。您是碩果僅存的捏麵人師傅嗎？

林先生：我不是最後一個捏麵人師傅，但妳說得沒錯——已經沒有很多人在做這行了。三十年前有好多捏麵人師傅，現在捏麵人已經是一項快要失傳的藝術。

梅：林先生，謝謝您和我談話。

03 與眾不同的清真寺 P. 24

位於馬利的傑內是世上一座最獨特宗教建築的原鄉。此建築稱為「傑內大清真寺」，其獨到之處為何？雖然多數清真寺均以木材或石塊所建，但這座清真寺卻以乾燥的泥土建成。

此座清真寺具有兩大特色。第一是外觀。棕色的清真寺，看似從周圍地面破土長出。第二就是清真寺的泥牆，必須由人民經常補修。而這就是此清真寺的外型逐漸改變的原因。事實上，補修工程對傑內人民而言是件大事。大家每年都會在「大清真寺塗泥節」期間，前來幫忙補修清真寺。

傑內大清真寺不僅獨特，還十分壯麗。世界各地的觀光客前來傑內只為一睹清真寺的樣貌。有些人是前來朝聖，有些人則是抱持欣賞藝術品的角度。還有些人單純想瞧瞧，世上規模最大的泥製建築是什麼樣子。

04 請投票給我！ P. 26

安妮將在這個學年競選年級學生代表。年級學生代表負責代表其所屬年級（或班級）的所有學生。這是一項非常重要的職務。年級學生代表需協助同學們的任何問題，將大家的想法轉達學校的領導人。年級學生代表亦需為同年級的學生籌辦各種活動與專案。還可能需要為這些活動與專案募款。

各年級學生每年都要投票選出年級學生代表。如果你想競選年級學生代表，就要製作自我介紹與政見承諾的海報。這樣所有學生才能了解應投票給你的原因。以下是安妮所製作的海報。祝安妮競選好運！

> 請投給
> **王安妮**
> 擔任八年級年級學生代表！
>
> 我承諾選上年級學生代表後，會實踐以下事項：
>
> 1. 要求學校週五開放穿便服！
> 2. 執行課後計畫，協助同學學習艱深科目！
> 3. 籌辦更多學校舞會活動！
> 4. 傾聽大家的問題，並尊重每個人！
>
> 感謝大家賜票！

05 健康的口腔，健康的身體 P. 28

不清潔牙齒，會導致牙痛。但還不僅止於此，口腔健康不佳還會對全身造成嚴重病痛！

細菌侵入牙齒的細小裂縫時，會開始孳生數量，很快就會腐蝕牙齒。使得牙齒裂縫變得更大，孳生更多細菌。不用多久的時間，牙齒就會開始出問題。

此情況會讓其他身體部位處於危險狀態。口腔的壞菌會進入血液，再經由血液前往不同的身體部位。例如進入心臟與大腦，然後造成損害。還會造成數種癌症。

60% 到 90% 的學齡兒童都有一些口腔健康問題。許多年輕人因為忽略此情況，而讓自己之後面臨嚴重健康問題的風險。因此，請定期且正確地刷牙、少吃甜食以及給牙醫師看診。這些簡單的做法，不僅能維持口腔健康，也能讓全身保持康健！

1-2 作者的目的及語氣／做出推測

06 全「氣」衝刺！ P. 30

蒸氣龐克時尚的奇妙世界

馬丁‧普林斯 撰 | 2021 年 6 月

回到 19 世紀，當時的人是如何想像 21 世紀的生活呢？也許他們會以為蒸氣可以做為一切的動力來源——從電腦到大型飛行器都是如此。而 19 世紀的服飾搭配未來「高科技」配件，又會是什麼樣子呢？我現在描述的風格就是「蒸氣龐克」。

而「蒸氣龐克」能為以下問題解答：「如果 19 世紀人所想像的未來成真呢？」雖然電影和小說常出現蒸氣龐克風格，但這樣的概念同樣存在於其他領域。如今，藝術家與設計師運用蒸氣龐克的概念，來創造令人驚艷的設計與服飾。

吉莉安‧格雷表示：「穿上蒸氣龐克風的時尚服飾，等於穿上古人的夢想。因此，蒸氣龐克時尚常給人一種奇怪又奇妙的感受。」（格雷是熱門蒸氣龐克時裝店「全氣衝刺」的店長。）格雷每年都會在店門口的街道上，舉辦蒸氣龐克時裝展。今年的秀展有吉莉安最喜愛的七名蒸氣龐克設計師共襄盛舉。

你想知道蒸氣龐克時尚是由哪些族群所創嗎？你想知道他們運用哪些工具和材料嗎？請翻到下頁一睹為快！

07 為摯友獻上最好的祝願 P. 32

親愛的蕾貝卡：

雖然我們不在同一個國家，但我仍要祝福妳生日大快樂！

妳會不會以為我忘了呢？才不可能。妳的生日是一個非常特別的日子。我記得我們第一次一起慶生時的事：有野餐，後來還下雨。我還病了好幾週！

今年很難熬，而無法陪伴我的好朋友，更令人難受。不過離開的決定是正確的，家人最重要。別擔心，我一直會在這裡等妳回來。我希望妳的奶奶能早日康復。

那今天在沒有我的情況下，妳會怎麼慶生呢？不管妳要如何慶祝，別吃冰淇淋配蛋糕。我們都知道結果會怎麼樣。妳絕對會因為半夜肚子痛而醒來。如果妳還是這麼做了，別說我沒警告妳喔！

祝妳有個美好的生日，蕾貝卡。妳是我親愛的朋友，我一直都掛念著妳。

愛妳的雅各

08 友善超商送的特別禮物 P. 34

詹姆士今天早上到「友善超商」買了零食。他結帳的時候，收銀員給他這張傳單和兩個「友善笑臉」貼紙。

「友善超商」非常重視我們的顧客。
今年四月，我們想向最忠誠的顧客致上最特別的謝意。

從 4 月 1 日至 4 月 30 日，來店消費每滿 30 元台幣，就能獲得一張「友善笑臉」貼紙。
收集友善笑臉即可獲得以下獎品：

10 個友善笑臉：可享以下任意產品打八折的優惠。

15 個友善笑臉：可享一杯咖啡半價的優惠。

20 個友善笑臉：可享一杯免費咖啡，或以下任意產品打五折的優惠。

25 個友善笑臉：可享驚喜禮物或以下任意產品免費的優惠！

30 個友善笑臉：可享驚喜禮物以及以下任意產品免費的優惠！

泡泡熊貓汽水	鱷魚巧克力棒
酸溜溜檸檬糖	甜蜜蜜蜂蜜蛋糕
多果汁柳橙汁	嘎吱先生洋芋片
米莉奶茶	爆爆莓果 QQ 糖
凍王巧克力冰淇淋	瘋堅果綜合堅果

所以，如果今年四月您想購買零食和飲料，別忘了來友善超商！

09 猴子專屬的大餐 P. 36

如果猴子會用月曆，牠們一定只會在十一月的最後一個星期天畫圈做記號。因為泰國的洛布里會在那天舉辦「猴子自助餐節」，讓猴子放鬆進行自己最愛的事：「吃東西」。

大家試著想像一下。在老舊寺廟廢墟之間佇立著白色的長形桌，有人打開桌上的餐罩後，就可看見五顏六色成堆的蔬果。幾百隻猴子從四處湧入跳上桌，直到飽餐到動彈不得，才會停止進食。

所以，當洛布里的猴子很好命。此城與猴子之間具有上千年的淵源。自助餐節則是比較近代的活動，是當地一名飯店業者於 1989 年帶動起來。他想透過這個方式對猴子「道謝」，以感謝猴子吸引遊客前來洛布里。

猴子自助餐節不僅是猴子的特別節日。許多遊客一樣會在自己的月曆上圈出這一天。那麼你還在等什麼？趕快訂機票和帶著相機，這是一場不容錯過的節慶！

群組： 琳恩　 菲　 傑瑞　 湯姆

琳恩：學校的才藝表演秀就在下週。我們要參加嗎？

湯姆：我們應該參加啊。對我們來說，是一個練習在觀眾面前演奏的最佳機會。

傑瑞：我覺得很好。

菲：我贊成。我們可以演奏幾首曲子？

琳恩：只能一首，所以要好好選。大家有想法嗎？

傑瑞：《悲傷星期天》怎麼樣？這首曲子我們演奏得很上手。

琳恩：確實如此，但《悲傷星期天》的節奏有點慢又哀傷，我想我們應該演奏比較有活力的曲子。

傑瑞：那麼《夏日趣》呢？我們可能需要多練習一下，但這是我們最活潑的曲子。

琳恩：很棒的點子，大家都贊成演奏《夏日趣》嗎？

菲：我贊成。

湯姆：嗯，我不曉得。

琳恩：為什麼不曉得呢？

湯姆：我只是覺得《悲傷星期天》比較好聽。

琳恩：但是不太適合這次的才藝表演秀！為什麼你老是這麼難搞呢，湯姆？

湯姆：好吧好吧，那就選《夏日趣》。

琳恩：很好。那我們就明天午餐到音樂教室一起練習。別忘了帶自己的樂器！

菲：好，明天見。

傑瑞：👍

湯姆：OK。

1-3　理解因果關係／釐清寫作技巧

收件人：莎拉、溫妮、琪琪、蘿拉
主旨：來我家開睡衣派對！

嗨，大家：

由於我這學期拿高分，所以我媽說我這週末可以開睡衣派對。

她說我可以邀請四個人，所以我想請四個最好的朋友來參加。

我們可以做很多好玩的事，例如看電影、吃零食，還有熬夜整晚聊天！

派對將從星期六晚上六點開始。我媽說她不想幫這麼多人下廚。所以我們可以從我家附近新開的披薩餐廳訂披薩!

我希望大家都能玩得盡興,所以請大家告訴我想做的活動。任何事都可以,這樣我們才能一起度過歡樂時光。

我媽還說,隔天早上她想帶我們去外面吃早餐。所以請告訴妳們爸媽,妳們會在星期天中午左右回家。

好!請在星期三以前,告訴我妳們會不會參加。這樣我才有足夠的時間做準備。

等不及要和妳們大家相聚!一定會超好玩!

莫莉

傳送

12 以綠植為夢想的獵人　P. 42

我們聽到「獵人」一詞,通常會聯想到動物。但是你是否知道也有植物獵人的存在?

植物獵人會追獵很難找到的植物。而且做起來比聽起來還難。因為此類植物可能生長於崇山峻嶺,或是洞穴最深處。所以必須具備獨特技能,才能勝任此職務。

舉例來說,植物獵人必須能夠在野外求生數日、甚至數週的時間。而且一定要會攀爬高樹與到達難以企及的地方。但最重要的是,一定要熟知植物。

洪信介具備上述所有技能。他高中沒畢業,卻自學了追獵植物的能力。而且他還是台灣最頂尖的植物獵人。只要具備動力、努力以及熱愛野外的心即可。

植物獵人可協助科學家尋找和研究罕見植物。他們還能追蹤每年永久消失的許多植物種類。令人難過的是,全世界有許多植物逐漸消逝,因此他們的工作比以往變得更加重要。

13 保持乾淨的海岸　P. 44

白沙灘淨灘活動

詳情　**活動主辦人:王瑪姬**
📍 白沙灘
🕐 6 月 3 日星期一,早上 8 點至 11 點
👥 目前有 15 人響應

請一起來幫助我們讓白沙灘保持乾淨!白沙灘是個很棒的去處,大家都愛在沙灘上放鬆或玩海灘遊戲。這裡也是兒童奔跑玩耍的熱門景點。不過,現在海灘上充斥了許多垃圾,包括寶特瓶、塑膠袋、紙杯和糖果紙。我們希望這個海灘能成為一個乾淨安全的場所,才能讓大家玩得開心。因此我們想找志工來協助撿拾海灘上的垃圾。

我們會提供垃圾袋與手套，還有零食和飲料。大家只要帶著你的人，以及一顆想要幫忙的心前來即可（或許也可以戴頂帽子，因為到時候會是大晴天）！

我們會在早上8點於海灘咖啡廳外集合。期待與大家相見！

14 推銷、推銷、買下去！　P. 46

你正要在網路購物，此時咖啡機的圖片旁突然出現一則訊息：「只剩最後一台！」你心想：哇！一定很好用，才會這麼受歡迎。是不是應該買呢？但其實你沒有很常喝咖啡……你還在思考的時候，又跳出另一則訊息：「目前有另外 20 人正在瀏覽此產品。」你覺得最好趕快買下去，以免別人捷足先登！所以，你很快就按下「馬上購買！」按鈕。

沒有計畫好就購物的行為，叫做「衝動購物」。這對許多購物者而言，確實是個問題。大家會花很多錢購買從來用不到的東西。而購物網站會運用許多聰明花招，來鼓勵衝動購物行為。包括促銷、熱賣商品標籤、星級評分與評價，還有限時倒數。

為了阻止自己陷入衝動購物，請在點下「購買」按鈕之前，先問自己幾個問題。我真的需要這件東西嗎？我會拿它來做什麼用途？我可以將這樣的金額拿來買哪些其他東西？切記，網路商店想要你的錢，所以會無所不用其極地要你花錢！

15 帶給地球的好消息　P. 48

蒂娜：那麼我們今晚的最後一則報導，對地球來說是個好消息。塑膠袋需要 150 年的時間，才能自然分解消失，因此會汙染我們的土地和海洋，但現在有一些友善地球的替代用品，正逐漸打入市場。我們的環保線記者詹姆斯·馬利，將報導這則新聞。交給你了，詹姆斯。

詹姆斯：謝謝妳，蒂娜。大家覺得我手上拿的是一般便宜的塑膠袋嗎？看起來是塑膠袋、感覺上也是塑膠袋。但事實上並不是用塑膠製成的，而是 100% 可生物分解的材質。用完之後，只要放在杯子裡並加入熱水，然後你就會親眼看見它消失不見！溶解後就能倒到水槽，不會留下有毒廢棄物，只剩下二氧化碳和水。如果這些新式袋子變得受歡迎，表示海洋裡的塑膠袋將有終結的一天。我們將現場交還給蒂娜。

蒂娜：謝謝你，詹姆斯。今天的時間就到此結束……

1-4 綜合技巧練習

16 課堂上的問題　P. 50

一位老師問了學生一個問題。以下是學生回應的內容：

茱莉亞：我常看到兒童在用，我覺得兒童還小，精力又旺盛，不該用這類設施的。我認為只有老人、身心障礙者和孕婦可以使用。

馬克：　我認為這類設施應該讓有需要的人都可以隨時使用。我常在公車和火車上感覺不舒服而想坐下來。我有一次真的病得很嚴重，當時是有一個空位，但我沒有坐下來，因為我覺得自己會被罵。

金：　　我不同意馬克的想法。如果任何人都能使用，那麼大家就會濫用制度。例如有人可以給個耍笨的理由，像是「我因為提了很重的包包，所以我要坐下來」。我覺得遵照原本的制度就好了。

格雷格：我認為乾脆完全取消這些設施和制度。多數人都很好心，如果看到有人需要坐下，就會讓座的。設置了這個設施，只會讓大家更有壓力。

17 我們能信任哪些新聞？ P. 52

媒體曾經很單純。如果想知道新聞，買份報紙就好。而且選擇不多，也許只有兩三家報社可挑選。而此類報紙會花錢請記者去外頭跑新聞。如果記者報導不實新聞，還可能丟掉工作。

網路改變了所有媒體生態。現在有許多新聞網站可選，而且很多網站還可免費瀏覽。這表示網站付不起記者的酬勞，那麼要如何拿到新聞？也許他們會從報紙或其他網站取得二手資訊，或是直接杜撰。

「假新聞」意指資訊不準確的新聞。有時是蓄意捏造，有時是單純出錯。但假新聞是個大問題。有時候甚至很難判斷孰真孰假。

那麼讀者該如何辨別假新聞？請一定要先思考一下網站的聲譽。媒體公司和記者十分在乎自己的聲譽。他們也許不一定都報導正確，但是不會故意欺騙讀者。

18 我們的動物需要您！ P. 54

我們的動物需要您！

您愛動物嗎？您超過 18 歲嗎？您每週至少有三小時的閒暇時間嗎？

「安全之家動物收容所」徵求幫手。

我們目前收留了超過五十隻貓犬，牠們需要許多照顧與關懷。
我們需要人手幫忙處理收容所的各項工作，包括以下事項：

>> 餵食動物　　　　　>> 陪貓玩
>> 維持收容所乾淨　　>> 幫動物餵藥
>> 遛狗　　　　　　　>> 在社群媒體發佈我們動物的文章

請注意：　我們的收容所沒有營利，因此無法支薪給幫手。但我們保證這項工作將令您大有所獲，這些可愛動物對您的喜愛，就是協助我們的回報。

如果您覺得這是自己想做的工作，請撥打 555-345-234 與我們聯絡，並留下資料。如果我們認為您是合適的幫手，將會回電給您。

19 爭取女孩就學的權利 P. 56

世上最貧窮國家有許多女孩無法就學，一位前世界領導人正試圖改變這個問題。

麗莎・斯壯 撰

茉莉亞・吉拉德曾是澳洲領導人，現在則是全球教育合作組織
（GPE）的領袖。該組織負責募款支持將近 70 個全球最貧窮
國家，GPE 主要致力於增進這些國家女孩的就學人數。

根據吉拉德的說法，許多貧困家庭在教育孩子時，均面臨
「非常棘手的選擇」。許多家庭的經費只夠送一個孩子去上
學。女孩則必須待在家幫忙做事，從未有機會去改善自己的
生活。

但是協助女孩就學，不僅對女孩本身有益。吉拉德相信，如
果女孩能就學和學習新知，國家就能更富裕、更安全且和
平。

請繼續閱讀，了解 GPE 的其他成功故事……

20 挺身發聲 P. 58

親愛的日記：

真是五味雜陳的一天，我都不知道該怎麼開始說。

我和平常下午一樣坐公車。車內非常擁擠。突然間，隔壁
的男子開始碰撞我，我甚至感到他的手在摸我的臀部。
這不是意外，他是在佔我便宜。

剛開始我動彈不得。我震驚又害怕。但很快就出現另一
種感受：「憤怒」。我轉過去面對這名男子。我看著他的
眼睛大喊：「變態，手拿開！」他很驚訝，他應該從未料
到，受害者會為自己挺身而出。

這個可怕的經驗會揮之不去很長一段時間，但也不全然
是壞事。這個經驗也有好的一面。例如其他人真的都想
幫我，有一個小姐甚至陪我走回家。而那個變態也沒逃掉，警方已經抓住他。

很高興我沒有姑息他，我對自己感到驕傲。我覺得勇敢發聲很重要。
也許很難做到，但至少你不孤單。

Unit 2 字彙學習

2-1 認識同義字與反義字／從上下文推測字義

21 別忽視我們 P. 62

現代世界的人生

陳雪莉

我去年去美國洛杉磯，當時我真不敢相信竟有那麼多街友。我上網查了一下，發現洛杉磯的街友超過四萬人！我在台北幾乎沒看過街友，我本來以為這在台灣不是一個問題。

後來上週我去台北車站逛購物商場時，發現有許多人——還是老人居多——睡在外面的街道。我真的很震驚。我搜尋研究了一下，發現台北有將近 650 名街友，當然這數字比洛杉磯少很多，但仍是存在的事實。

我很好奇，所以我買了便當，送給其中一個街友。我開始和他聊天，想了解他的故事。他 57 歲，未婚無子。他曾在工廠工作，五年前失業後，就找不到其他工作。他只有等到年滿 65 歲，才能領政府的救濟金。我問他，大家該怎麼做，才能幫助到台灣的街友。他說：「別忽視我們。」

22 非洲文化的重要環節 P. 64

成為靈體：我跨入非洲面具世界的旅程

■ 序言 ■

我 13 歲參加博物館校外教學之旅時，第一次見到非洲面具。它擁有紅與金的色彩、大大的空洞眼神與長長的下巴。有好幾個月的時間，我都忘不了那張臉，就像對我施了魔咒一樣。所以我決定盡我所能的了解非洲面具。

在這麼多年中，我讀遍各種關於這個主題的書籍。我得知面具在許多非洲部落的儀式中，扮演重要角色。它們代表許多事物——包括亡者、動物或是神話傳說中英雄的靈體。人戴上面具後，就不再是人類，而成為了面具之靈。

我學習越多，就越想深入了解。但為了真正了解此類面具的奧秘，我清楚必須親自到非洲拜訪面具的製作者。我必須親眼看見大家使用面具的模樣。而這本書記錄了這趟旅程的故事以及我的發現。

23 封城下的生活 P. 66

現在是 2020 年 12 月。住在英國的理察，正在與台灣的朋友琳打視訊電話。

理察：嗨，琳！哇，真開心能看到妳！

林：嗨，瑞秋！我也很開心！妳那邊的新冠肺炎疫情怎麼樣呢？

理察：我們這裡在封城，所以我無法和任何朋友碰面。而且幾乎所有商店和餐廳都關門了，但我沒有生病，所以至少這是件好事。

林：我很高興聽到妳健康的消息。那妳的爸媽還好嗎？

理察：我爸很好。我媽昨天開始咳嗽，所以她自己在房間隔離，不能出來。她很快就要去檢測，我們就會知道她有沒有感染病毒。

林：我希望她沒事。如果商店都關門，你們如何取得食物？

理察：超市還是有開，所以必要時，可以去採買食物。但我們必須戴口罩，進入超市時，要和大家保持遠一點的距離。

林：聽起來真是難熬，我希望妳那邊的一切能很快好轉。

理察：我也希望。嘿，我們來聊聊比較不悲慘的事吧。妳新養的貓還好嗎？

林：她很好！我叫她過來——莫莉，來這裡，莫莉！

24 造訪法國的機會 P. 68

公告

交換學生計畫

2021 年 12 月 1 日

明年三月到四月，七年級學生將可參與交換學生計畫。3 月 7 日至 3 月 14 日，法國保羅拉皮耶大學的學生將來訪本校。而本校學生則從 3 月 28 日至 4 月 4 日前去造訪保羅拉皮耶大學。這是認識不同文化以及和母語人士練習法文的大好機會。

法國學生來訪期間，會寄宿在本校學生家中。而本校學生參訪法國期間，則寄宿於法國學生的家中。

如果大家想報名此計畫，請於 12 月 14 日之前找珍維爾老師報名。此計畫僅開放 15 個名額，因此請儘快報名，以免向隅。不過切記，請務必事先取得家長的同意！

謝謝大家
奎爾老師
現代語言科主任

25 停止那些「嗯」和「啊」 P. 70

我們說話時常會使用「嗯」、「啊」、「就像是」和「你知道的」等用字措辭。這些語詞雖沒有任何意義,卻有助於繼續對話。然而,如果你準備要向聽眾演講,應該試著擺脫此類用詞。

應擺脫此類用詞的兩大原因如下:第一,你對大眾演說時,通常是要表達重要的訊息。用虛詞呈現演講內容,會讓你的訊息聽起來不夠有力。第二,此類語詞讓人很容易分心。如果你的聽眾察覺到你一直在使用此類語詞,就會無法專注於你要傳達的訊息上,而會花時間等著聽你說出下一個「就像是」或「嗯」。

為了破除這個習慣,你可以練習放慢講演速度。我們的嘴巴常常動得比思緒快。所以,我們在用「嗯」等字時,表示思緒正在趕上說話。公開演說的時候,請從容不迫,試著不要緊張,你的演說內容就會比較流暢,聽眾也會更清楚聽見你的訊息。

26 蜜蜂的住所 P. 72

社區公告

協助我們的本土蜜蜂!

你知道多數蜜蜂並不會和幾千隻其他蜜蜂一同住在蜂巢裡嗎?沒錯,九成的蜜蜂其實都是獨居,牠們不會製作蜂蜜,還很少攻擊人類(因為沒有需要保護的蜂巢!)。因此牠們不會危害寵物和人類,還可協助重要的糧食作物授粉。沒有牠們,許多糧食就無法生長。

令人傷感的是,此類蜜蜂正在消失。牠們和我們一樣,都喜歡擁有私人的小空間。牠們喜歡居住在窄長型孔洞,類似竹孔中。我們這種乾淨的現代化建築與整齊的花園,並無法提供許多地方給牠們居住。

但是我們可以伸出援手!製作特殊的蜜蜂旅館很簡單。只需要幾種簡單的材料和基本工具即可。如果你想打造蜜蜂旅館,請來橡樹路 4 號找我。我備有各種必需品,來教大家如何建造!

感謝大家幫助當地蜜蜂!

約翰・史密斯

27 擁有最艱難工作的狗狗 P. 74

狗狗是很棒的寵物,而牠們也是優秀的學習者。因此,我們常訓練牠們來協助我們做事。其中最勤奮工作的狗就是警犬。警犬身負許多重要職責。牠們負責搜索毒品和炸彈,協尋失蹤人口,還能保護警官不受攻擊者的傷害。

許多犬種均非常適合擔任警犬，不過目前最受歡迎的是比利時馬利諾犬。馬利諾屬於身形瘦長且強壯的中型犬，而且跑得很快，活力充沛與專注力高。因此可說是擔任艱難警務的完美「犬」選。

警犬的訓練過程十分艱難且耗時。警犬最終必須能夠在毫不遲疑的情況下服從主人。訓練結束後，警犬可服役高達九年的時間再退休。退休時，常會跟隨原本的主人同住。有些國家政府還會每年給予補助金，來支付照顧牠們所需的開銷。我們真的虧欠這些努力工作的狗狗太多。因此，在牠們晚年時，善待牠們真的很重要！

28 愛之樹 P. 76

德國一座森林裡，生長著一棵樹幹洞的 500 歲橡樹，洞裡塞滿了世界各地的人所寫的信。

大家稱此樹為「新郎橡樹」。19 世紀時，米娜・歐赫特與威漢・舒特費什這兩個當地年輕人深愛彼此，但米娜的父母不同意兩人結婚。因此他們開始秘密通信，將森林裡的橡樹當作藏信處。米娜的父親最終讓步讓兩人結婚，因此他們在 1891 年 6 月 2 日，就在這棵特別的樹下共結連理。

這對幸福佳偶的故事傳開後，大家開始寄信到這棵樹。這些寄信人希望能有人找到他們的信，讀信後並回信，希望藉此找到真愛。1927 年，當地郵務單位在樹旁設置梯子。郵差開始正式送信到這棵樹。如今，仍有很多尋愛的人會寫信，會定期送達新郎橡樹。

29 忙碌工作的一週 P. 78

吉姆是一名消防員。以下是他日記中的一頁。

3 月 12 日

今天很平靜。早上我們接到一通電話，因為有隻貓卡在樹上下不來。貓咪十分緊張，還試著抓傷我。還好我有戴著厚手套！

3 月 14 日

今天有座古宅失火，有位媽媽用油烹飪的時候著火了。我們雖然撲滅火勢，但已造成許多損害。幸好那家人很快逃離失火的住宅，沒有人受傷。

3 月 16 日

今天是個悲傷的日子。高速公路發生一起重大車禍。我們必須鋸開車體拉出一名女子。雖然我們行動迅速，但她仍受到重傷。救護車已載她前往醫院，希望她康復。

3 月 18 日

今天是個好日子。我前往一所學校，向學生宣導消防安全知識。他們都很專心聽，我想他們獲益良多。往後他們如果遇到失火情況，就會知道該怎麼做。

30 尊重彼此的不同意見 P. 80

午安。

我今天的演講主題是「讓自己受不了的事」。我們不會總是認同每件事。也許你討厭我最喜歡的電影，也許我覺得你的鞋子跟你的服飾不搭。但如果要說有件事我們經常能達成共識，那就是「我們都有各自受不了的事」。

舉例來說，誰喜歡見到有人張大嘴吃東西的樣子？沒人想看到你嘴裡的食物。但這種情況卻屢見不鮮！

另一個讓人受不了的常見現象就是「插嘴」。我們都知道這種人就是不讓你講完自己的事。最糟的是：他們從來就補充不了任何寶貴資訊。插話內容通常類似「我也看過那部電影！」好棒棒，但有需要這麼急著告訴我嗎？

最後，還有些人總是愛遲到。例如你想看最新的賣座強片，你買了電影票，但有個朋友從不準時出現。而且不只這樣，你還得在電影院外等候，才能把電影票交給他。

你受不了的事也許和我不一樣。但我們都有受不了的事。而這樣的共同點，能讓我們凝聚在一起。

感謝大家。

Unit 3 ：學習策略

3-1 影像圖表

31 吃美食、寫見聞、發文章！ P. 84

你喜歡美食嗎？你喜歡拍攝美食嗎？你有寫作才華嗎？那麼你或許可以成為美食部落客！美食部落客會前往許多不同餐廳，在個人部落格上寫下經歷。亦可能評價街頭小吃、特別的零食和美食節活動。

成為美食部落客是件很有趣的事！但這一樣需要勞心勞力。多數的美食部落客均單獨工作，所以必須獨自處理每件事。他們要拍攝所有照片，撰寫所有文字，要管理自己的網站，還需要謹慎計劃時間。但是辛勤工作就會得到很棒的回報。成功的美食部落客，能讓自己的部落格獲得幾百萬的點擊率，並在美食圈裡佔有重要地位！

請看下頁行事曆所列的一位美食部落客忙碌的行程範例。行事曆會顯示星期和日期，你可以在每個星期或日期新增「待辦事項」，還有預計執行的時間。

珍娜的美食部落格行事曆

2022 年 5 月 第一週

星期日	星期一	星期二	星期三	星期四	星期五	星期六
1 中午 12 點 小房子餐廳 晚上 7 點 班的披薩屋	**2** 早上 8 點 陽光早餐咖啡廳 下午 2 點 王先生牛肉麵	**3** 寫作日	**4** 下午 1 點 多汁大漢堡 晚上 9 點 老街夜市	**5** 早上 11 點 漂亮粉紅甜點店 下午 5 點 咖哩王印度餐廳	**6** 寫作日	**7** 下午 1 點 到 6 點 格林公園的日本美食展

32 很遠很遠的村莊 P. 86

七海愛丁堡是特里斯坦庫涅小島上的唯一村莊，此島位於非常遙遠的大西洋中部。島上沒有機場。想前往該島，必須先從南非搭船，且需要六天的航旅時間。而最鄰近的居民，則是住在 2,173 公里以外的另一個聖海倫娜島。因此，這表示七海愛丁堡成為了地球上最偏遠的村莊。

但對 250 名居民而言，七海愛丁堡就是他們的家園。請看下頁的地圖。地圖是某地的簡圖。這張地圖上有標號。右邊的圖框說明每個號碼代表的建築。你可以看到學校、醫院和兩座教堂。而島上的人為了謀生，會耕作、捕魚或到海邊的小龍蝦工廠工作。

是的，這裡是世上最遙遠的地方，但是在此偏遠村莊的生活，卻也沒有太大的不同。

33 追蹤我！ P. 88

亨利喜歡用手機拍照。他會自拍、拍他的愛貓、他的食物、他的親朋好友——無所不拍！他最近開了一個 IG 帳號。剛開始都沒有人追蹤他，但短短五天後，就有 104 個追蹤者！亨利很有興趣知道，哪類照片的追蹤者會最多。因此接下來五天，他仔細地做記錄。

他早上發了一張新照片。然後睡前記錄一下總追蹤人數。第一天，他發了一張戴太陽眼鏡的自拍照。第二天，他發了有美味湯餃的午餐照片。第三天，他發了自己和朋友去海灘的照片。第四天，他發了愛貓「咪咪」和玩具老鼠的照片。第五天，他發了奶奶在廚房的照片。

請看一下數據的折線圖，並回答以下問題。線圖會以點狀符號來顯示數字。然後將所有的點連成線，你就能看清楚經過一段時間後的數字變化。

亨利的 IG
總追蹤人數

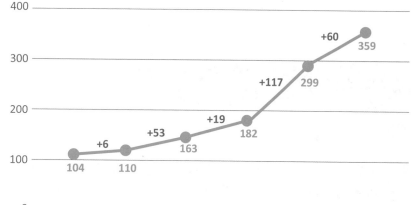

折線圖數值：
104　+6　110　+53　163　+19　182　+117　299　+60　359

剛開始的追蹤人數　第一天結束　第二天結束　第三天結束　第四天結束　第五天結束

34　在週末販售點心 P. 90

安妮最近開始了自己的餐車事業，生意目前不錯，但安妮的問題是餐車滿小的。有時特定品項很早就賣光，她想知道哪些品項會在哪一天賣得好，這樣她就能帶更多這類品項，而不會太早就賣光。

為了理清頭緒，上週末安妮以長條圖（下圖）記錄每日銷售量。長條圖能以不同大小和顏色的長條顯示數據，因此可輕鬆比較不同的數據。

安妮的餐車銷售量 週五至週日

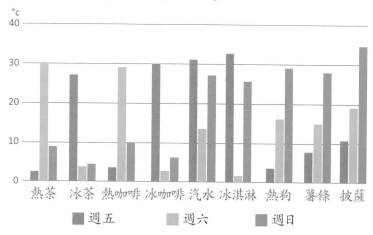

熱茶　冰茶　熱咖啡　冰咖啡　汽水　冰淇淋　熱狗　薯條　披薩

■ 週五　　■ 週六　　■ 週日

安妮亦做了天氣方面的筆記。週五的天氣炎熱晴朗（氣溫：攝氏 32 度）；週六則下大雨且寒冷（氣溫：攝氏 13 度）；週日風和日麗，晴朗但卻舒服涼爽（氣溫：攝氏 18 度）。

有了這份資料，安妮現在更能好好地為下週生意做好準備。

35　水都到哪裡去了？ P. 92

居家用水量

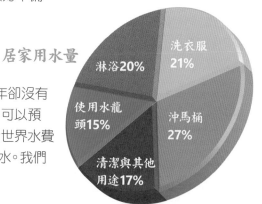

洗衣服 21%
淋浴 20%
使用水龍頭 15%
沖馬桶 27%
清潔與其他用途 17%

台灣快缺水了！台灣多數的水來自颱風，但 2020 年卻沒有颱風襲擊本島。而氣候變遷讓全世界變得更乾燥，可以預期的是，未來台灣的颱風會越來越少。台灣也是全世界水費最便宜的一個地方，因此，大家常不經思考就浪費水。我們務必要從現在開始改變壞習慣！

那麼我們每個人該怎麼做才能節約用水？請看下頁的圓餅圖。圓餅圖會以圓形裡的數塊扇形圖來標示數據。扇形圖越大，表示數據越大。你相信我們大部分的家庭用水都消耗在沖馬桶嗎？而節約用水的其中一個絕佳辦法，就是用水桶收集淋浴的水來沖馬桶，這樣就可以將用水量降低至超過四分之一！如果大家一起省水，就能讓台灣的未來免於旱災！

3-2 參考資料

36 你有太多東西嗎？ P. 94

你的房間亂七八糟嗎？也許是時候斷捨離你的人生！「斷捨離」意指丟掉你不需要的東西。擁有較少的物品，對思緒和情緒都好。但是斷捨離不大容易。幸好，有許多書籍會教你如何幫房間斷捨離。下頁列出麗莎・馬克林的此類著作《少即是好》的目錄。目錄會顯示一本書的每章名稱，亦提供每一章的頁數。有了麗莎的一點幫忙，你也能斷捨離個人環境。

37 遊戲機大戰簡史 P. 96

第一台家用電玩遊戲機於 1972 年問世，名稱叫做「美格福斯奧德賽」，售價約 600 元美金。這樣的花費能讓你擁有什麼？你只有 28 種遊戲可玩，而且多數遊戲都非常簡易，難怪只有 35 萬人買單。

在那個時代，電玩遊戲完全是新玩意兒。打電玩的原因不在於超好玩，而是因為它們很奇特（也就是說，你也不見得有機會玩到）。早年沒有很多人擁有電玩遊戲機。

如今，從你的好友到奶奶，人人都在打電玩。無論是智慧型手機或電玩遊戲機，我們都愛玩。打電玩曾經是一件奇怪的事，現在是不玩的人才奇怪。試想看看：PlayStation 4 的時代賣出超過 1.15 億台遊戲機，比美格福斯奧德賽還要多太多了！

請看看以下的年表。年表會依照時間最早到最晚的順序列出事件。此年表則列出部分熱門的電玩遊戲機以及問世的日期。

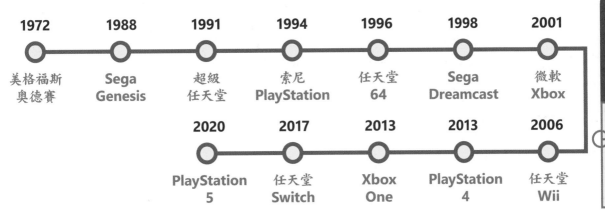

1972	1988	1991	1994	1996	1998	2001
美格福斯奧德賽	Sega Genesis	超級任天堂	索尼 PlayStation	任天堂 64	Sega Dreamcast	微軟 Xbox

2020	2017	2013	2013	2006
PlayStation 5	任天堂 Switch	Xbox One	PlayStation 4	任天堂 Wii

Translation

UNIT 3 學習策略

38 攪拌！微波！美味出爐！ P. 98

布朗尼是我最喜歡的點心。這款甜點香甜、可口又能輕鬆在家製作！你通常需要一台烤箱來做布朗尼。不過台灣人的廚房不常有烤箱，所以我要怎麼做我的布朗尼呢？我使用的是微波爐！

只要具備幾種簡單食材、一台微波爐和一個杯子，就可以在家做出好吃的布朗尼。請看一下下頁食譜！食譜會列出食材，並且一步一步告訴你某菜色的製作方式。

用杯子微波製作布朗尼

總時間：少於 5 分鐘
份量：1 份

食材

乾料
- 麵粉（30 克）
- 糖（50 克）
- 可可粉（2 大匙）
- 鹽（一小撮）
- 肉桂（一小撮）

濕料
- 水（60 毫升）
- 融化的奶油（30 毫升）

裝飾配料
- 冰淇淋／糖粒／棉花糖／草莓

製作步驟

步驟 1：將乾料加到杯子裡拌勻。
步驟 2：加入濕料拌勻。
步驟 3：在微波爐裡烹煮 60 秒。（如果微波爐的火力不是很強，可能需要烹煮久一點。）
步驟 4：等布朗尼冷卻後，再加上裝飾配料。
步驟 5：開吃！

39 許多同義字 P. 100

英語的單字很多。雖然不可能知道到底有多少，但我們認為至少有 25 萬個！當然，你不需要學會所有單字！約有 9,000 個單字涵蓋了 98% 的日常英語，但此數量還是很多！當你在學這些單字時，將意思相近的單字分組在一起有助於你學習。

以 hard 這個單字為例。有哪些其他單字的意思等於 hard？difficult、challenging、tough 都是。還有其他同義字嗎？我們一起查同義詞辭典就能找到答案！同義詞辭典就是充滿同義字（意思相同的單字）的書籍，同義詞辭典甚至還會列出反義字（相反意思的單字）。每一個條目都會依照字母順序（從 A 到 Z）列出同義字與反義字。

hard

1. *形* 難以進行或了解
同義字：baffling, challenging, complex, complicated, difficult, impenetrable, intricate, involved, problematic, puzzling, tough, tangled,
反義字：clear, easy, simple

2. *形* 不柔軟
同義字：compact, dense, firm, inflexible, rigid, solid, strong, tough, unyielding
反義字：flexible, malleable, pliable, soft

40 怪物殺手！ P. 102

你知道《鬼滅之刃》嗎？這是一部非常熱門的日本漫畫與動畫影集，描述一位年輕男孩竈門炭治郎的故事。一日，惡鬼殺了他全家，並把他妹妹也變成了惡鬼。炭治郎承諾要殺了惡鬼讓妹妹變回人類。

此部漫畫可說是史上最賣座的連載漫畫，而第一季的動畫影集便榮獲許多獎項。超受歡迎的《鬼滅之刃》電影亦於 2020 年上映。你還有興趣了解更多資訊嗎？如果要查找更多《鬼滅之刃》的消息，只要在網路搜尋引擎搜尋「鬼滅之刃」即可。你在搜尋時就會看到如下列所示的搜尋結果，每條結果均顯示網址和該網址的部分資訊。

www.toottoot.com/demon-slayer-season-1
線上看第一季鬼滅之刃
馬上註冊 TootToot，即可觀賞多集鬼滅之刃和其他熱門的電視節目。第一個月免費……

www.animestore.com/demon-slayer-kimetsu-no-yaiba
出售鬼滅之刃玩具和服飾
鬼滅之刃 T 恤與帽子，還有所有你喜愛的鬼滅之刃角色公仔——炭治郎……

www.demonslayerfans.com
鬼滅之刃大全
歷史｜故事｜角色｜漫畫｜動畫｜電影 --- 此網站由鬼滅之刃粉絲專為鬼滅之刃粉絲所建置。大家可在此查找各種資訊，包括漫畫作者到……

www.fivestars.com/demon-slayer-mugen-train

鬼滅之刃——丹·夏普的影評—— ⭐⭐⭐⭐⭐

我是鬼滅之刃動畫的鐵粉,所以當我聽到有電影版的時候,我超興奮。大家猜怎麼著?我好愛這部電影!電影一開始……

www.tvnews.com/demon-slayer-season-2

鬼滅之刃第二季即將上架——我們目前已知的訊息

熱門的鬼滅之刃動畫影集第二季即將上架!新一季影集將於兩週內開播。我們電視新聞網站會透露與往後故事情節有關的特別資訊……

Unit 4 綜合練習

4-1 閱讀技巧複習

41 真正的偉大女性 P. 106

凱薩琳二世是俄羅斯最偉大的一位領袖,1762 年掌權,統治俄羅斯達 34 年之久,直到 1796 年去世。

凱薩琳在位期間成就許多大事。儘管她並未生於俄羅斯,仍十分愛國,希望看見俄羅斯變得富強蘊含文化。

凱薩琳深信教育的力量,她認為只有人民的思想進步,俄羅斯才會變得強大。因此她著手推行全俄羅斯教育制度的現代化。1786 年,她在全國建立上百所免費學校,開放不論貧富的男女入學。她亦支持許多藝術家和科學家,因此在位時的俄羅斯藝術與科學均蓬勃發展。

此外,凱薩琳巧妙地並用外交與戰事手腕,大幅擴大俄羅斯領土,直至去世時俄羅斯已掌控了大面積的歐洲東南部,甚至包括部分的北美地區。

俄羅斯在凱薩琳的統治下,成為歐洲最強大且重要的一個國家,因此,羅斯人現在都稱她為「凱薩琳大帝」!

42 戴好口罩! P. 108

https://www.stayhappyandhealthy.com

<u>首頁</u> > <u>新冠肺炎</u> > <u>口罩</u> >

由於新冠肺炎疫情仍未獲得有效控制,因此戴好口罩非常重要。戴上口罩就是保護自己不會得病。但更重要的是,如果你已經確診,口罩能防止你傳染給別人。為了確保口罩能發揮效用,請務必正確戴上口罩。許多人不知道該如何正確戴口罩,讓口罩變得無用武之地。

正確戴口罩的 **7** 個步驟

1. 戴上口罩前，請先好好洗手。
2. 確保將白色那面的口罩向內，有色的那面向外。
3. 將掛繩拉到耳朵上戴好。
4. 口罩必須罩住口鼻，並且下拉罩住下巴。
5. 下壓口罩的鋼條，以便服貼於鼻子。
6. 確保口罩不會太鬆垮。如果太鬆垮，請將口罩掛繩調短一點。
7. 確保你能順暢呼吸。如果覺得呼吸困難，可能需要使用較大的口罩。

43 太辣了嗎？再也不是問題！　P. 110

我和很多人一樣，都愛吃辣！問題在於灼燒感有時真的會讓我受不了！我的嘴巴好像著火似的！只想冰水一杯接一杯地喝，但是似乎沒有奏效。我必須痛苦地坐著，等到灼熱感消散，眼看其他人繼續享受美食！

不過，科學家已經知道我這痛苦的問題可以如何解決——那就是牛奶！
辣椒充滿了辣椒素，這就是造成我嘴巴灼熱的原因。而辣椒素不溶於水，
所以不論我喝多少水，辣椒素還是會停留在我的舌頭上，但辣椒素卻會溶解
於牛奶。所以如果我喝一口牛奶，就能沖掉辣椒素，嘴裡也不再有灼熱感。除牛
奶以外，含糖量高的飲料亦有相似的效果。

現在我知道了解決辦法，就再也不會因為吃太辣而受盡折磨了！我終於可以盡情享用辣味美食！

44 照顧多肉植物的法則　P. 112

你知道多肉植物嗎？它們是一種很美的植物，能點綴房間。你也應該種一盆！不過如果你開始種多肉植物，請確保好好照顧它。以下列出部分實用的小技巧：

❶ 將多肉植物放在晴朗的地方，每天需要日曬大約六小時。

❷ 時常幫此植物移動方向，才能確保多肉植物的每一面都能獲得足夠的日曬。

❸ 水澆在泥土，不要澆在葉片。

❹ 保持植物乾淨，葉片上如果太多灰塵，會使多肉植物難以生長。

❺ 確保花盆底下沒有積水。

❻ 使用正確的泥土，確保泥土不會保留太多水。

❼ 別讓蟲蟲吃掉你的多肉植物！泥土保持乾燥可有效驅蟲。

❽ 不同季節的澆水量需不同。多肉植物會在春季生長，在秋季和冬季休眠。關於澆水只要記得口訣：「春季澆多點，秋季澆少點」。

45 超越笑容與彩色制服的表象 P. 114 ....

你能想出一些高風險的運動嗎?你大概會想到美式足球或冰上曲棍球這類運動吧?絕對不會是啦啦隊,因為那只是漂亮美眉熱舞的運動而已,不是嗎?請三思喔!

啦啦隊是一項非常需要認真以對的活動,女隊員常需要完成離地好幾公尺的艱難特技。男隊員則必須將女隊員高舉在空中,還要在她們落地前安全接抱住。而且,他們還必須一邊做特技,一邊為觀眾展現出最亮眼陽光的神情。因此,啦啦隊員需要非常強壯,還要具備絕佳的平衡感和專注力。一個動作錯了,就會導致隊員受重傷。

因此,啦啦隊可說是是最危險的一項運動。女性運動員的嚴重意外中,超過半數都是發生在啦啦隊。所以,雖然啦啦隊看起來是很有趣的活動,但絕對不適合膽小的人。這不僅是一項面帶笑容與身穿彩色制服的活動,而是真的具有危險性的艱難運動!

46 青少年適合的工作? P. 116 ....

周馬丁
1 天前發布

我剛看了這部有趣的影片。我很認同影片的想法。我很喜歡青少年時期有份工作的感覺。大家覺得怎麼樣呢?

影片: 青少年為什麼應該工作 [10 分鐘]

💬 **13 則留言**

王羅伊
我今年十五歲,我真的很想找份工作。因為我想自己賺錢來買想要的東西。但我媽媽不讓我工作。

> **魏蒂娜**
> 王羅伊 我同意你媽媽的看法。台灣的學生必須為準備考試而讀書,他們沒有時間兼顧一份工作。

> **陳吉娜**
> 魏蒂娜 連一份兼職工作都沒時間做嗎?週六或週日工作幾小時,不會太影響學生的學業。

珍妮・瓊斯
美國青少年找工作是正常的現象。工作能教會他們獨立。我認為這是正面的事。

瑞克・史密斯
我 15 歲的時候,我爸叫我去餐廳找份工作。當時我很討厭工作。我只想待在家打電動。
不過,這份工作確實教會我一些很好的人生道理。

瑞秋已經進入高中最後一年。她最近寄出一些大學申請書,其中一所大學請她參加簡短的面試。以下是面試官提問的一些問題,以及她的回應內容。

面試官: 妳為什麼對這所大學感興趣呢?

瑞秋: 數學是我最喜歡的科目,我最近讀了葛蕾絲·瓊斯教授的著作《數字的魔法》,她就在這所大學任教。我認為她的想法十分引人入勝,我希望能成為她的學生。

面試官: 妳覺得高中的哪一個科目最難學?

瑞秋: 歷史。要記下所有不同日期真的很難,但我制定了一種讀書方法來幫助自己。我會為每一個歷史事件寫一首簡短有趣的歌曲,這樣就能輕鬆記下日期。

面試官: 妳會用什麼方法來讓我們的大學變得更美好?

瑞秋: 我很喜歡現場音樂,所以我希望能協助籌辦音樂會。我覺得音樂會是一個讓學生交新朋友的良好環境。

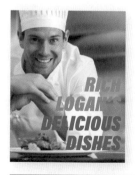

瑞奇·羅根的美食
瑞奇·羅根 撰

★★★★★

電視節目《超級主廚》冠軍,為大家帶來超過 100 道的美味食譜。

馬上購買 15.99 美元

書評

「每一位認真的居家料理人,都應該擁有這本書!」

——《家廚雜誌》

「瑞奇·羅根熟知讓簡單食材變得美味的方法!」

——《美食世界》

「這本書裡有世界各地的菜色,包括法國、中國、印度、義大利、英國等更多國家。如果你想學會各種豐富料理,這本書非常適合你!」

——《每日新聞書評》

「本書的每道食譜均使用簡單的食材,且易於上手,所以非常適合初學者。不過經驗老道的廚師,也一樣能學到一些酷炫的新技巧。」

——《每月優食》

「雖然經驗老道的廚師都熟悉這些菜色,但羅根為每道菜色加入了自己特別的新意。儘管我已經是資深廚師,仍躍躍欲試想試做每道食譜。」

——倫敦「王子餐廳」主廚,戴瑞斯·布朗

49 鯨魚只是一種大魚嗎？ P. 122

鯨魚和魚類長得相似，而且共享相同的水下家園。大家曾以為牠們是同一種動物，但我們現在已知道真相：牠們完全不同。

為了瞭解牠們有多不同，請看看下頁的文氏圖。文氏圖有兩個圓圈。此文氏圖將鯨魚的事實資訊列在左邊的圓圈，魚類的事實資訊列在右邊。而兩個圓圈重疊的部分，就是鯨魚和魚類共有的事實資訊。

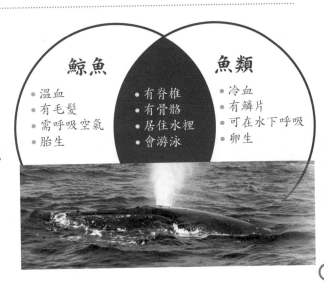

鯨魚
- 溫血
- 有毛髮
- 需呼吸空氣
- 胎生

有脊椎 / 有骨骼 / 居住水裡 / 會游泳

魚類
- 冷血
- 有鱗片
- 可在水下呼吸
- 卵生

鯨魚是胎生動物，還會照顧寶寶多年。魚類會產下成千上萬顆卵，然後繼續過自己的生活。魚卵孵化時，沒有人會來保護魚寶寶，因此高達 99% 的魚寶寶會在長大前就死亡了。

鯨魚亦需要呼吸空氣，這點和魚類不同。牠們雖然住在水中，但仍需要浮出水面呼吸。那麼鯨魚可以憋氣多久？這必須視鯨魚種類而定。虎鯨每分鐘都會浮出水面，但抹香鯨可以憋氣 90 分鐘。

因此，或許比較好的問題是：鯨魚是否和人類一樣？

50 每個單字的故事 P. 124

我們都知道，各國有歷史，各種建築也有其歷史。但你知道單字也有歷史嗎？有些單字歷史十分令人驚訝呢！

以英文單字 tea 為例，大家知道這個單字的由來嗎？17 世紀時，歐洲多數的茶葉來自中國福建省的廈門和台灣。茶葉抵達歐洲

時，大家開始問這是什麼東西，賣家就用泉漳語（台語）介紹「tê」。到了西班牙，此單字變成了「té」；到了法國變成「thé」；而到了英格蘭，就變成「tea」！

大家可以購買與單字歷史相關的許多書籍。多數此類書籍的後面都有索引表（請看下頁範例）。索引表會依照字母順序（從 A 到 Z）列出本書的重要主題。如果想查找某個主題，只要翻閱索引表，尋找主題，然後翻到該頁碼閱讀即可。

我們的單字來自哪裡？

索引表

Answer Key

Unit 1　閱讀技巧

	1.	2.	3.	4.	5.
1	1.B	2.C	3.D	4.B	5.A
2	1.D	2.A	3.D	4.C	5.A
3	1.D	2.A	3.B	4.B	5.D
4	1.B	2.D	3.A	4.C	5.C
5	1.C	2.A	3.A	4.A	5.D
6	1.D	2.A	3.C	4.A	5.B
7	1.D	2.A	3.C	4.A	5.C
8	1.B	2.D	3.C	4.B	5.C
9	1.C	2.A	3.A	4.B	5.D
10	1.D	2.A	3.C	4.C	5.C
11	1.D	2.B	3.A	4.D	5.C
12	1.B	2.A	3.D	4.D	5.C
13	1.B	2.C	3.A	4.C	5.A
14	1.B	2.D	3.B	4.A	5.B
15	1.C	2.B	3.A	4.A	5.C
16	1.D	2.A	3.C	4.B	5.C
17	1.A	2.B	3.D	4.D	5.C
18	1.B	2.A	3.D	4.B	5.C
19	1.C	2.A	3.D	4.C	5.B
20	1.B	2.A	3.C	4.B	5.D

Unit 2　字彙學習

	1.	2.	3.	4.	5.
21	1.D	2.B	3.A	4.C	5.B
22	1.A	2.C	3.D	4.D	5.B
23	1.A	2.D	3.D	4.A	5.B
24	1.D	2.B	3.C	4.D	5.A
25	1.A	2.D	3.B	4.A	5.C
26	1.C	2.D	3.B	4.A	5.D
27	1.C	2.A	3.B	4.D	5.B
28	1.B	2.B	3.B	4.C	5.A
29	1.D	2.A	3.C	4.D	5.C
30	1.B	2.D	3.A	4.B	5.C

Unit 3　學習策略

	1.	2.	3.	4.	5.
31	1.D	2.B	3.A	4.C	5.D
32	1.A	2.C	3.B	4.D	5.B
33	1.A	2.B	3.D	4.A	5.D
34	1.B	2.A	3.A	4.A	5.C
35	1.B	2.B	3.A	4.C	5.D
36	1.A	2.B	3.C	4.D	5.D
37	1.B	2.D	3.C	4.D	5.B
38	1.C	2.A	3.D	4.C	5.D
39	1.B	2.A	3.D	4.C	5.B
40	1.D	2.A	3.B	4.D	5.C

Unit 4　綜合練習

	1.	2.	3.	4.	5.
41	1.C	2.B	3.A	4.C	5.D
42	1.B	2.A	3.B	4.A	5.A
43	1.A	2.D	3.B	4.D	5.C
44	1.B	2.B	3.B	4.C	5.B
45	1.D	2.A	3.D	4.B	5.C
46	1.A	2.C	3.D	4.B	5.A
47	1.D	2.A	3.B	4.D	5.B
48	1.B	2.D	3.D	4.D	5.C
49	1.C	2.B	3.B	4.A	5.C
50	1.D	2.D	3.A	4.C	5.B

讀出英語核心素養

2

九大技巧打造閱讀力

作者	Owain Mckimm
協同作者	Zachary Fillingham (3, 7, 9, 12, 17, 20, 30, 37, 44, 49)
譯者	劉嘉珮
審訂	Helen Yeh
企畫編輯	葉俞均
編輯	楊維芯
主編	丁宥暄
內頁設計	鄭秀芳／林書玉
封面設計	林書玉
發行人	黃朝萍
製程管理	洪巧玲
出版者	寂天文化事業股份有限公司
電話	02-2365-9739
傳真	02-2365-9835
網址	www.icosmos.com.tw
讀者服務	onlineservice@icosmos.com.tw
出版日期	2023 年 8 月 初版再刷（寂天雲隨身聽 APP 版）(0102)
郵撥帳號	1998620-0 寂天文化事業股份有限公司

國家圖書館出版品預行編目 (CIP) 資料

讀出英語核心素養：九大技巧打造閱讀力.
2(寂天雲隨身聽 APP 版)/Owain Mckimm 作；
劉嘉珮譯 . -- 初版 . -- 臺北市：寂天文化事業股
份有限公司 , 2021.05
　面；　公分
ISBN 978-626-300-014-8(平裝)

1. 英語 2. 讀本

805.18　　　　　　　　　　　　110006432